are to be returned on or before
last date below.

TEA-LEAF ON THE ROOF

William's dad is Justin Case, famous author of mystery stories for children. But William's dad's stories have little to do with life in Tettiscombe Terrace where William lives. Nothing ever happens in Tettiscombe Terrace and William thinks it is the most boring place on earth!

But then something does happen — a thief nicks all the lead from the roofs and leaves everyone with leaking attics. William's dad is furious, but William and his friends are delighted. A tea-leaf on the roof! Here is their chance to do a bit of detective work of their own and beat the police to it. But it's not as easy as they think and they soon find detective work taking some rather unexpected turns . . .

ABOUT THE AUTHOR

Jean Ure is one of the most distinguished authors writing for teenagers and children. She had her first novel published when she was fifteen and still at school, but spent two years at drama school and had a variety of jobs before turning to writing full-time. She has now written many highly-acclaimed novels.

Jean Ure lives in Surrey with her husband, two cats and three dogs.

TEA-LEAF
ON THE ROOF
JEAN URE

HEINEMANN
NEW WINDMILLS

Heinemann Educational Books Ltd
Halley Court, Jordan Hill, Oxford OX2 8EJ
OXFORD   LONDON   EDINBURGH
MADRID   ATHENS   BOLOGNA   PARIS
MELBOURNE   SYDNEY   AUCKLAND
IBADAN   NAIROBI   HARARE   GABORONE
SINGAPORE   TOKYO   PORTSMOUTH NH (USA)

ISBN 0 435 12358 0

First published in 1987 by Blackie and Son Limited
First published in the New Windmill Series 1990

94 11 10 9 8 7

Cover design by The Third Man
Cover illustration by Tracey Agate

Printed in England by Clays Ltd, St Ives plc

William's Dictionary of Cockney Slang

apples and pears	stairs
ball of chalk	walk
barnet fair	hair
boat race	face
brahms and liszt	drunk
bread and honey	money
cat and mouse	house
cream crackered	knackered
currant bun	sun
daisy roots	boots
deaf and dumb	bum
dickie dirt	shirt
dog and bone	phone
english rose	nose
frog and toad	road
german bands	hands
gypsy's riddle	piddle
half inch	pinch
hampstead heath	teeth
holy ghost	toast
jam jar	car
king lear	ear
loop the loop	soup
lucy locket	pocket
lupino lane	rain

marie corelli	telly
mince pies	eyes
mutt and jeff	deaf
north and south	mouth
pen and ink	stink
plates of meat	feet
plum duff	rough
pot and pan	old man
rabbit and pork	talk
rosie lee	tea
skin and blister	sister
taties in the mould	cold
tea-leaf	thief
t'mater loop	soup
titfer tat	hat
trouble and strife	wife
vicar of bray	tray
weasel and stoat	coat
whistle and flute	suit
wooden plank	Yank

1

'Very well done, you kids! You beat us to it! If it hadn't been for you,' said Sergeant Trotter, 'the villains might never have been caught . . . I shall recommend you all for a share in the reward . . .'

Sergeant Trotter beamed his congratulations. The kids—the two big ones, Alistair and Eliza, the middle one, Dorothy, and the two little ones, plump Porky and tiny Spickanspan—beamed back. They had done it again! They had solved the mystery of the burnt-out car . . .

William snorted.

'Huh!' he said. He tossed the book contemptuously across the bedroom floor. It lay there, face down, in the middle of the rug: *The Mystery of the Burnt-Out Car* by Justin Case, with a picture of the five revolting children. Plump Porky and tiny Spickanspan . . .

William made a being-sick noise over the side of the bed. Incredible to think there were some kids, somewhere, who actually enjoyed reading Justin Case. William only read him because he had to—because short of contracting a fatal disease he couldn't think of any way of avoiding it.

Justin Case was William's father. Justin Case wasn't his real name—his real name was Gavin Potter. He had chosen Justin Case because he thought that kids would be amused by it. William wasn't, but then William had to live with it.

With a sigh, he humped himself off the bed, retrieved *The Mystery of the Burnt-Out Car* and took it across to his bookshelf to go with all the others. They were all mysteries; Justin Case didn't write anything else. There was *The Mystery of the Great Bank Robbery, The Mystery of the Pink Toad, The Mystery of the Runaway Train*—that had been a particularly soppy one. All these kids racing up and down the country after an international gang that had hijacked this very special train that had a member of the royal family on board.

Honestly! It was pathetic. How could you admit to your friends that you had a father who wrote stuff like that? It was about time Gavin realized that things just didn't happen in real life like they happened in his books—or if they did, then kids weren't allowed within a million miles of them. It was always, 'You shove off, you kids, or I'll have the law on you!'

It was the Jogger's favourite cry: 'You shove off, you kids!' He had yelled it at them only yesterday, when all they had been doing was testing the door of his car to see if it was burglar-alarmed. You'd have thought he'd have been *grateful*. Serve him right if someone came and burgled it off him in the night.

Fat chance! William stared moodily out of the window. Nobody ever came burgling in Tettiscombe Terrace, probably because they knew there wasn't anything there worth burgling (apart from the Jogger's car, and it *was* burglar-alarmed—it had shrilled for ten minutes before he had found a way of stopping it).

Once upon a time, back in the days of Queen Victoria, Tettiscombe Terrace had been known as the Pride of Tettiscombe. It had been new, then, and very grand: six tall, narrow houses standing in a row, with a gravelled drive for carriages and a thick hedge of yew to screen it from the road. Now it was run-down and seedy, the brickwork crumbling, the gravelled drive a sea of mud, the yew hedge all begrimed with petrol fumes and stuck about with empty Coca-Cola cans and beer mugs from the pub. It was what Gavin described as 'come down in the world'.

It was coming down for good just as soon as the Council could rehouse everyone. Most people had already gone up to the new estate on Monksfield. There were only a few of them left, now, scattered about the Terrace. There were Chalky White (who was William's hero) and Alec Masterson (otherwise known as the Jogger) at number one; the Potters at number three, the Richardsons at number four; the art students at number five and the Khans and old man Coppins, down in his basement, at number six.

The Potters lived on the top floor plus attics. One of the attics was William's bedroom, the other was Gavin's study. From his window William could see across the road, to the shops opposite (all boarded up) and the chimneys of the power station in the distance. Alistair and co. didn't have to live in attics and look out on power stations. They lived in the country, near 'a bustling market town, with the quaint old name of—'

'William!' From the floor below, Sue's voice called up to him. Sue was William's mother. 'Do you want anything to eat?'

'The quaint old name of *Wynken cum Warde*.'

'And could you please knock on Gavin's door and tell him it's tea time?'

William pulled a face; partly at Wynken cum Warde, partly at the thought of knocking on Gavin's door. Gavin had just started Chapter One of a new mystery: he tended to be rather touchy if disturbed on a Chapter One. William decided not to bother him. He didn't fancy getting shouted at.

He thudded down the attic stairs, banging with his feet on the linoleum so that if Gavin happened to be asleep (which he sometimes was) he would get woken up, and went through into the kitchen.

'Did you tell him?' said Sue.

'He's busy.' And if he wasn't, then he jolly well ought to be.

'So what are you going to eat?'

Mentally, William consulted his dictionary of Cockney slang. (The dictionary was a secret project that he was working on. So far he had collected forty-three entries, most of them gleaned from Chalky. When he had a hundred he was going to send it to Gavin's publisher and surprise everyone by getting it published.)

'I'll have . . . cuppa Rosie, t'mater loop 'n two bits o' holy ghost.'

Sue looked at him. 'You couldn't speak English, could you?'

He could; but he was trying to teach her Cockney slang. She didn't seem to be making much progress. Sternly, he translated: 'Rosie Lee, cuppa tea; t'mater loop, t'mater soup; holy ghost, bit o' toast.'

'Thank you,' said Sue.

After eating his loop and ghost and drinking his cup of Rosie, there didn't seem much else to do. Six o'clock on a sunny summer evening, the first Sunday of the holidays, and here he was at a loose end . . . the kids in Gavin's books were never at a loose end. There was always some villain to chase or some mystery to solve.

He clumped his way down three flights of uncarpeted stairs, the empty house echoing to the slap-slop of his trainers on the worn linoleum, let himself out through the front door with its stained-glass panels, and wondered where to go.

Usually at six o'clock on a Sunday he'd have called round for Mash, at number six, and they'd have gone out the back together to kick a ball or dig for bodies, but the Khans had driven up to Leicester for the weekend and wouldn't be back until late.

If it had been Saturday he could have thumped on the wall of his attic and rapped out a message to Charlotte; but not on a Sunday. The

Richardsons went to church on Sunday. They went once in the morning, and then again in the evening, in a big blue transit van which collected lots of other black families from round and about and drove them to the church on the corner of Station Road. The transit van was there now, waiting.

Further along the Terrace, the Jogger was cleaning his car. The Jogger was always cleaning his car. It was a Fiat Regata, dismissed scornfully by Gavin, who couldn't afford a car at all as 'a heap of tin'. William didn't think it was a heap of tin, exactly, though if he'd been given the choice he would sooner have had Chalky's Thunderbird—even if it *was* a bit rusted here and there. The Fiat was all brand new and shiny, like a little polished egg; but who in their right mind would want a polished egg when they could have a splendid shocking-pink monster which snorted and roared and belched great black clouds of smoke?

The Jogger glanced up as William approached. His forehead instantly knitted itself into a network of suspicion.

'What do you want?'

'Don't want anything,' said William.

'So what are you doing here?'

'Just standing.' Nobody could stop you just standing. There wasn't any law against standing.

'Just so long as you don't touch my car again,' said the Jogger. 'If you touch my car again I'll tan your ruddy hide.'

William stood watching him, gravely.

8

'Do you understand?' said the Jogger.

'Yes,' said William; but in self-defence he added: 'We were only testing it.'

The Jogger made a hissing sound.

'I don't want it tested! It doesn't need testing—especially not by your grubby little paws! You can do what you like with that load of crap—' he jerked his thumb contemptuously over his shoulder towards the Thunderbird—'but just keep away from my Fiat!'

'Here!' A figure rose up, indignantly. 'Who's that calling my jam jar a heap of crap?'

The Jogger started, and almost dropped his polishing rag—he obviously hadn't realized that Chalky was there.

'You take that back!'

Chalky advanced threateningly, wielding a greasy spanner. The Jogger's pinched lips became even more pinched than usual.

'There is no need for violence,' he said.

'You take it back, then! Else I'll duff you one.'

William waited breathlessly. He wouldn't half mind seeing the Jogger being duffed one.

'What you said about my jam jar,' said Chalky. 'You take it back!'

'Oh, for crying out loud!' The Jogger gave a final flick with his polishing rag. 'Let us not descend into brutality over a mere car.' He turned, and stalked off across the drive to the steps of number one. There he paused, to glare at William. 'Just you remember,' he said. 'Any more touching and you'll get a clout round the ear!'

9

The Jogger disappeared through the door. Chalky lowered his spanner.

'You hear that? What he said about my jam jar?'

William nodded, sympathetically. 'Yes, and it's a much better jam jar than his. My dad says his jam jar's just a heap of tin.'

'Yeah. That's right. Heap o' tin.'

Chalky kicked at one of the wheels of the Fiat. It didn't do the wheel any harm: Chalky's feet, as usual, were clad in old tattered trainers held together with string. His hair, yellow and a bit strawlike, was tied into a bunch at the back of his neck—the bunch was also fastened with string. Chalky's hair fascinated William. Everything about Chalky was fascinating—his yellow hair, his tattered trainers, the gold earring that he wore in one ear; and, of course, his wonderful, shocking-pink Thunderbird, which drove everyone but William mad with its throbbing and roaring.

Once, on one never-to-be-forgotten occasion, Chalky had taken William for a burn-up in it. They had burned all the way to the Elephant and Castle and back, with the radio going full blast so that they could hear it above the noise of the engine. People had stood in the street and shouted as they roared past, and an old lady had poked at them through the window with her umbrella while they were revving up at some traffic lights and demanded to know whether they were deaf.

William stood for a bit, while Chalky did things under the bonnet with his spanner. Then

10

Chalky straightened up and said, 'Well, I reckon that's about it for now, then, John.' (Chalky always addressed William as John. William had been puzzled at first, he had kept saying, '*William* . . . my name's *William*,' but in the end he had worked out that John was just another way of saying mate.) He liked the thought that he was Chalky's mate. 'Reckon I'll be knocking off now.'

'You doing things?' said William.

Chalky said yes, he was going back up the old apple and pears to wash his boat, then popping down the frog and toad for a quick couple of pints before coming back to watch the old Marie Corelli and crash out early, "Cos I'm right cream-crackered.' (By which William understood that he was going upstairs to wash his face, then popping down the road for a quick couple of drinks and coming back to watch the television before going to bed early on account of feeling knackered.)

'See ya,' said Chalky.

With Chalky gone and Mash not back, there really didn't seem very much point in staying out. He might just as well go home and work on his dictionary. (Marie Corelli: telly. That was a new one.)

He made his way back to number three along window ledges and the tops of steps, pretending there was a hundred foot drop into a burning fiery furnace on one side of him. It was Sue who came down to let him in. She said, 'Oh, good! I'm glad you're back. Gavin's got a chapter he wants to read to us.'

Just for a minute, William thought that the burning fiery furnace would almost have been preferable. At least if you fell into a furnace the agony would be over quickly. When Gavin read one of his chapters it went on for hours—well, it seemed like hours—and even when he'd finished it wasn't really over because then he expected you to make bright comments. He grew very tetchy if you didn't have something intelligent to say.

Glumly, William followed Sue up the stairs. As they reached the top landing she turned and winked.

'Don't worry! We'll have a game of battleships afterwards.'

Afterwards seemed a long time away. The chapter looked ominously bulky to William. There were pages and pages of it.

'If you're ready?' said Gavin.

'We're ready,' said Sue. She turned, brightly, to William. 'We're looking forward to it, aren't we?'

'Yes,' said William.

Gavin cleared his throat. '*The Mystery of the Stuffed Banana* by Justin Case. Chapter One: The Banana Goes Missing.'

'Oh! This sounds like fun,' said Sue.

Gavin glowered at her; he didn't care for interruptions.

'Sorry,' said Sue.

'Chapter One,' said Gavin. He readjusted his spectacles, cleared his throat again and began: 'Alistair and co. were starting to grow restless. It was time they had another mystery to solve!

The last one had been the case of the burnt-out car, when Sergeant Trotter had recommended them all for a share in the reward—but that had been weeks ago!

'"All the villains seem to have gone away on holiday," grumbled Eliza.

'"It's ages since we had a really good mystery on our hands," agreed Porky.

'"I wish something exciting would happen," piped Spickanspan.

'"*I'd* like to catch some international drug smugglers," volunteered Dorothy.

'"Personally, I'm getting so bored," Alistair informed them, "I wouldn't even mind just bagging an ordinary common-or-garden thief."

'"Imagine if a burglary happened in our own house," giggled Eliza. "That would be something!"'

It would be something, thought William glumly, if anything at *all* ever happened in Tettiscombe Terrace.

2

Something had happened in Tettiscombe Terrace! The roof had sprung a leak ... not just one leak, either, but lots and lots of leaks.

There had been rain during the night, and William's attic was soaked through. What was worse, so was Gavin's. In William's attic there was only William; but in Gavin's attic there was Gavin's typewriter and Gavin's plots file and Gavin's ideas notebook, not to mention Chapter One of Gavin's precious new manuscript.

The plots file and the ideas notebook had fortunately only got a little damp at the edges, but the typewriter was awash and the precious manuscript had gone all limp and soggy. Gavin was beside himself.

'My manuscript!' he kept saying. 'My manuscript!'

'It'll dry,' said Sue. 'Try putting it in the oven.'

'In the *oven*?' Gavin's eyes popped behind their spectacles. 'My *manuscript*?'

'Why not?'

Gavin glared, indignantly. Sue, who was used

to Gavin's glares, took no notice but went on busying herself about the kitchen, snatching at bits of breakfast in her usual early-morning rush to get off to work.

Gavin went on fuming.

'It should never have happened! It's a disgrace!'

'Well, don't tell me,' said Sue. 'Tell the Council.'

'I will,' said Gavin. 'Don't you worry! First thing after breakfast—'

'William, here's your Rosie.' Sue's hand went snaking overhead with the teapot. Gavin ducked, just in time. 'If you want any ghost—'

At last! She was learning!

'—you'll have to get it yourself. Right? I'll see you this evening.' Sue snatched up her bag and ran. From the top of the stairs they heard her calling: 'Don't forget to hang those bedclothes out!'

The reason the bedclothes had to be hung out was that some of the rain, in fact quite a lot of the rain, had actually splattered onto William's bed. No wonder he had been lying there having dreams about being in a swimming bath! The rain had come in in great gollops. Gavin said the roof must have been in an appalling state and that the Council obviously hadn't looked at it for years. He said it was 'absolutely typical' and that sharp on the dot of eight-thirty he was going to ring them up and give them a piece of his mind.

Sharp on the dot of eight-thirty he did so.

William, munching his way through burnt ghost and runny honey, listened with interest.

15

Gavin was pretty good at giving people pieces of his mind. In William's opinion, he was better at that than he was at writing mysteries.

'. . . absolute disgrace,' said Gavin.

The voice at the other end of the line appeared not to agree with him. William heard it, faint and far away. It sounded somewhat truculent.

'Bleep blop blurp blee. Bleep bleep blurp. Bleep bloop bla. Bla.'

'Look, I am telling you,' roared Gavin, 'that we have been rained on!'

'Bla?'

'My typewriter has been rained on! My *manuscript* has been rained on!' Mentally, William added: 'My son has been rained on.' 'My livelihood is at stake!'

'Bloo blo blaw. Blee bloo?'

'Don't you give me that!' bellowed Gavin. 'You sit up there, in your ivory tower—'

William dipped a bit of burnt ghost into the honey. Gavin sounded as if he were having trouble.

'. . . *immediately*,' snapped Gavin. 'Or else.'

He slammed the receiver back down.

'Else what?' said William.

'Or else,' said Gavin, 'I shall be forced to do something unpleasant!'

William sat forward, eagerly.

'What'll you do?'

'I shall write to my MP,' said Gavin.

Write to his MP? 'Is that all?'

'What do you mean, is that all? Get on with your breakfast! And don't talk with your mouth full.'

William chewed and swallowed.

'S'what about the Council?'

'What about them?'

'Aren't they going to do anything?'

'They are sending someone round,' said Gavin. 'Immediately,' he added.

'Will they have ladders? Will they go up through the skylight? Can I go up there with them?'

'No, you cannot!' yelped Gavin.

'It's quite safe,' said William. 'It's flat as flat. Anybody could just go up there quite easy. Even you could—'

'I said *no*,' said Gavin. 'Go and get your bedclothes and hang them out like you were told.'

'*I* wasn't told,' said William. 'Not me specially. We both was. She meant both of us. She—'

'Do it!' snarled Gavin.

He was obviously in one of his moods. It never did to argue with Gavin when he was in one of his moods. Huffily, William stomped back up the stairs. It was enough to make a person sick! All these books about kids driving runaway trains, kids grappling with armed criminals, kids diving into burning buildings and Gavin wouldn't even let his own kid just get up on a perfectly flat roof and have a quick look. That was all he wanted, just one quick look. He bet from up there you could see practically the whole of Tettiscombe.

He pulled, grumpily, at the top sheet. This was a jolly exciting way to start the summer holidays, hanging out bedclothes. He bet old Alistair never had to hang out bedclothes. Alistair seemed to spend his entire life witnessing bank robberies and giving chase to villains. You never heard of him doing any of the ordinary, boring things like going shopping or cleaning his teeth.

With the bedclothes slung over his shoulder and wound round his neck to keep them from trailing on the ground, William clattered down the stairs, out through the back door into the garden, and slunk off through the undergrowth towards Sue's clothes line at the far end. It would have been easier, of course, to use the path, but that way he could be seen (imagine being *seen* hanging out wet bedclothes) and in any case he was being an explorer tracking through the tropical rain forests with a boa constrictor wrapped round his neck.

He was just trying to decide whether it would be more fun for it to be a tame boa constrictor, or one that had dropped on him from a great height and was slowly crushing him to death, when there was a sinister swishing sound from somewhere behind and a black furry shape suddenly sprang on him and pulled him to the ground.

For a moment he thought it might be a ferocious, man-eating panther but it was only Boy, the Richardsons' large, shaggy mongrel.

William struggled to sit up. If Boy were there, then Charlotte couldn't be far behind; and Charlotte was the last person he would like to have watching him as he hung out wet sheets (especially sheets that were only wet in *patches*).

'Gerroff!' he said to Boy, who was smothering him even more effectively than the boa constrictor had done.

Too late! Charlotte's feet, in their bright red trainers, were already crashing through the jungle towards him. Charlotte's voice came shrieking self-importantly: 'We've been *rained* on!'

'So've we,' said William, fighting his way out through mounds of fur.

'It's come through all over.'

'I know,' said William.

'It's wetted all the attics,' squeaked Geraldine. 'There's a huge enormous puddle in the middle of the floor!'

Geraldine was Charlotte's sister. She was seven, the same age as Spickanspan. William and Charlotte were eleven.

'It's gone all down our wall,' said Charlotte, meaning her and William's wall, the one they rapped their messages on.

'It's got all over my bedclothes,' said William.

He said it rather anxiously, wanting her to know. 'That's why I'm having to hang them out. 'Cos they've got wet. In patches.'

He needn't have worried—Charlotte was far too interested in her leaking roof to take any notice of William's wet bedclothes.

'My mum's been on to the Council,' she said.

'So's Gavin,' said William, yanking at one end of a sheet which seemed somehow or other to have found its way into Boy's mouth. 'They're sending men round with ladders to go up there and do something. I'm—' he tugged at the sheet. Boy tugged back. With a loud ripping sound, the sheet tore up the middle. Sue wasn't going to be happy about that. 'I'm going to go up there with

19

them,' said William. He gave one last tug. 'Going to go up through the skylight and have a look round.'

Charlotte said that she was going to go up through the skylight and have a look round as well. Geraldine, who didn't even know what a skylight was, said that she was, too.

'It was my idea,' said William.

Charlotte looked at him. 'So what?'

So she didn't have any right to come barging in, that was what! If too many of them did it, there wouldn't be any glory attached.

'Don't expect they'll let you, anyway,' he said. 'It's not a woman's thing.'

'You looking for a punch-up?' said Charlotte.

She would, too, Charlotte was so butch.

Mash, when they went round to his place, hadn't heard about the rain coming in. The attics in his place had been empty for months.

'F'r all you know,' shouted William, 'you could be flooded!'

'It could be coming down the stairs right now,' shouted Charlotte.

Eagerly they ran up to look, but it seemed the roof wasn't leaking at this end of the Terrace. There wasn't a damp patch to be seen. The others were disappointed, but Mash said that it was 'Just as well, really. My father stores things up there ... he gets cross enough if you just try looking, even. He'd go spare if it got rained on.'

'My mum went spare,' said Charlotte. 'She got on to the Council and tore strips off 'em.'

'Gavin *swore*,' said William.

'So did my mum . . . she said they didn't seem to care if we rotted.'

'Gavin said they were a load of lazy lay-abouts.'

'Immediate,' said William. 'Gavin said if they didn't come immediate he's going to do something unpleasant.'

'Like what?'

'Like going down the Town Hall and bashing 'em.'

'That's what my mum's going to do,' said Charlotte. 'She's going to go down and bash 'em, an' all.'

William's chest heaved, indignantly. He bet Mrs Richardson wasn't going to do anything of the sort.

By half-past eleven, the people from the Council had still not arrived. Gavin had appeared several times on the front steps looking furious, and Mrs Richardson had joined him and agreed that it was a disgrace. Boy, having nothing more sensible to do, had overturned all the dustbins, Geraldine had climbed into the yew hedge and fallen out of it again, the other three had thrown rocks at a Coca-Cola can, played hop-scotch in the mud, and collected car numbers till their eyes were dizzy. Charlotte now declared that she was fed up with waiting for people who never came and she was going to go up the adventure playground instead. Geraldine said so was she. Mash hesitated, looking at William.

'You coming?'

Sternly, William shook his head. 'Can't. Someone's got to give a hand.'

'Dunno what use you think you'll be,' jeered Charlotte.

'More use'n you would!' said William.

He didn't know why it was he had all this trouble with Charlotte. All this lip. Alistair never had to put up with it from his two. Eliza and Dorothy behaved properly, as girls should.

The others went off. William stayed where he was. He was being a soldier on guard. A soldier couldn't desert his post. It was a matter of honour.

Unfortunately, Gavin didn't seem to understand about matters of honour because at twelve o'clock he came downstairs and curtly told William that instead of sitting there 'cluttering the place up' he could do something useful: 'You can go down the road and collect some library books.'

'Can't,' said William. 'I'm at my post.'

'What post? What are you talking about?'

'My *post*,' said William. 'Like in *The Mystery of the Black Horse,* when Alistair stayed on guard day and night at the entrance to the bank, waiting to catch the bank robbers—'

'Yes, yes, yes!' said Gavin. 'I know all about that, I wrote it. You just shift yourself . . . go on!'

Resentfully, William shifted. He couldn't recall Alistair ever being made to desert his post just to go running errands for parents. As a matter of fact, Gavin always took jolly good care to see that Alistair and co. weren't bothered by parents. They always spent the first one hundred and nine pages of a book being lost in plane

22

crashes over the Andes or given up for dead in the Burmese jungle.

Just at that moment William could have wished that Gavin were given up for dead in the Burmese jungle. It had been his ambition to get on that roof ever since he had discovered that you could climb onto it through the skylight—*if* you had a ladder. Gavin and Sue didn't have one. He'd tried standing on a chair, but it was nowhere near high enough. He'd be jolly furious if he went and missed his chance just because of Gavin and his boring old books.

Coming back from the library, William turned into the drive of Tettiscombe Terrace. He stopped. There outside the steps of number four was the little blue van that belonged to the Council. Parked next to it was another vehicle—a car with blue and red stripes which belonged to the police.

Slowly he raised his eyes to the roof. Figures were moving to and fro. Some were Council workmen, some were unmistakably Old Bill.

William set off at a run. At the far end of the drive he could see Chalky White, about to start up in his Thunderbird.

'Hey!' yelled William. 'What's going on?'

Chalky stuck his head out of the car window.

'Naffing tea-leaf on the roof, John . . . nicked all the naffing lead.'

3

A tea-leaf on the roof! William could hardly believe his luck. A tea-leaf—in Tettiscombe Terrace!

A tea-leaf admittedly wasn't in quite the same class as a bank robber or an international jewel thief, but still it was better than nothing. After all, everyone had to start somewhere.

As Chalky pulled away in his usual cloud of smoke, William turned and galloped off excitedly down the drive. Gavin had now appeared. He was standing at the foot of the steps of number three with Mrs Richardson. Both of them were looking upwards, shading their eyes against the sun.

'There's bin a tea-leaf!' shouted William. 'Tea-leaf on the roof!'

'Yes,' said Gavin. 'We know.'

'Gone and nicked all the naffing lead!'

'Yes,' said Gavin. 'We know.' He turned, and transferred his gaze to William. 'Who told you?'

'Chalky,' said William.

'That long-haired layabout! How did he get to hear of it?'

'Spec' the p'lice told him.'

'The police,' said Gavin, grandly, 'have spoken with no one save myself—and, of course, Mrs Richardson.'

'I s'pose they're up there looking for clues?' said William. Looking for footprints and things; for some mark of identity left behind by the villain. Villains always left something behind. In *The Mystery of the Pink Toad* it had been a keyring with a set of keys. Alistair and co. had discovered it tucked beneath the carpet after the police had failed to spot it. The police in Gavin's books usually did fail to spot things. Sergeant Trotter had rather ruefully commented on it in *The Mystery of the Burnt-Out Car*: 'You kids obviously have extremely sharp eyes.'

William had sharp eyes. He could read the numbers on buses even when they were still way down at Tettiscombe Grove. Sue couldn't; neither could Gavin, even with his glasses. So if there *were* any clues—

'What are you looking so happy about?' said Gavin.

'It's like in one of your books,' said William. *'The Mystery of the Great Roof Leak.'*

Gavin gave a short laugh.

'There's no mystery about it! Some anti-social joker got up on the roof and stripped all the lead, it's as simple as that.'

'I just hope when they catch them,' said Mrs Richardson, 'they're made to pay for all the damage they've done.'

Gavin shunted his glasses further up his nose.

'They'd be birched, if I had my way.'

'What's birched?' said William.

'Thrashed,' said Gavin, 'in a word.'

Villains in Gavin's books were never thrashed. Alistair, being rather saintly, always managed to find excuses for them (even though he handed them over to the police so that the police could put them in prison). William sought in his mind for a possible excuse for the lead-nicker. He was hampered by the fact that he wasn't really sure what lead *was*. The only lead he had ever come across was the lead used in pencils. Maybe the tea-leaf was out of work and wanted the lead to start up a pencil factory.

He put the suggestion to Gavin.

'What are you on about?' said Gavin. 'Pencil factory!'

It was Mrs Richardson who explained that the lead used in pencils wasn't the same as the lead used on roofs. The lead used on roofs came in sheets (sheets like bed sheets? William grappled with the idea) and was put there to stop the rain coming in.

'So what would they want it for? If they weren't going to make pencils out of it ... what'd they do with it?'

'Flog it,' said Gavin. 'Straight down the nearest scrap yard.'

'What, you mean they'd get money for it?'

'Unless they're totally brainless—which of course they may well be. Anyone that goes out stripping roofs in the pouring rain obviously needs his head examined.'

'P'raps when he got up there the rain hadn't

started?' said William. 'P'raps he'd already made arrangements to go tea-leafing, and the rain took him by surprise.'

Gavin looked at him, distastefully. 'Whose side are you on?'

'I'm just trying to understand,' said William. He wanted to get things clear in his mind. Someone had gone up on the roof and stolen all these sheets of lead so that he could take them round to the nearest scrap yard and get money for them.

'How'd they get it there? In a suitcase?'

Mrs Richardson said, 'No, darling. It's far too heavy to go in a suitcase. More like they'd have had a truck, or something.'

'And how much'd they get for it, d'you reckon?'

'Too much,' said Gavin.

'Ten pounds? Hundred pounds?'

'A lot,' said Mrs Richardson. 'There's a lot to be made out of scrap.'

William thought about it. He was still trying to see it in his mind's eye ... all those sheets, all stiff and white, folded into creases, like after Gavin had done the ironing.

'What exactly *is* scrap?' he said.

'Junk,' said Gavin.

'Like in old man Coppins's?'

'I beg your pardon?' said Gavin.

'I said, like in old man Coppins's? Like he has down in his b—'

'How old are you?' said Gavin.

'Eleven,' said William. He said it indignantly. Fancy a father not knowing a thing like that!

'And how old, do you suppose,' said Gavin, 'is

27

Mr Coppins?'

'Dunno.' Nobody knew how old old Coppins was. Nobody in living memory had ever seen him. Mash had a theory he was a vampire and only emerged at dead of night to suck people's blood. He was really creepy, living down there in the darkness.

'Well, I'll tell you,' said Gavin, 'he's a good bit older than eleven . . . so for the future it might perhaps show rather more respect if you were to refer to him as *Mr* Coppins. And instead of just standing here you can take those library books up to my study for me. Then I suggest you go and open a tin and start getting some lunch.'

'But I want to stay!' said William. 'I want to stay and see the p'lice!'

'Yes, and I want to have my lunch! I've already been interrupted quite enough for one morning. Just do as you're told—and show some respect!'

With deep bitterness of heart, William stumped his way back up the stairs. It was just as he had known it would be! The minute anything happened it was, 'You shove off you kids! Nothing to do with you!' That was typical of grown-ups. They wanted to hog all the excitement for themselves. Well, they weren't jolly well going to keep *him* out of it!

Quickly, William darted up to the attics, dumped Gavin's books on his desk, scuttled back down to the kitchen, stuck a loaf of bread and a block of cheese on the kitchen table and raced back outside. He was just in time to see one uniformed police officer and a plain clothes detective (he had to be a detective if he was plain clothes—William had learnt that from Gavin's books) come walking round the side of the Terrace, from the direction of number six.

Gavin and Mrs Richardson stood waiting for them. William, crouched at the top of the steps behind one of the door pillars, heard Gavin's voice say: 'So what did you find up there, officer?' and the detective reply: 'Not a lot, sir. Whoever did it, did a good job . . . stripped the place bare, except for the one at the end.'

'Oh! Ran out of pop, did he, by the time he got there?'

'Either that, or—' The detective paused, significantly. 'Anyone living in the attics at number six, sir?'

'No, they're empty. Been empty for months.'

'Ah. Well, in that case the chances are he simply couldn't handle any more. He'd already got a car load. We discovered where he's been dumping the stuff— over the side of number two, straight down onto the garden. You can see the marks where he humped it round to the getaway vehicle.'

Getaway vehicle! William's heart swelled. This was bigger stuff than he'd realized.

'I take it, by the way, that number two has been completely vacated? Yes . . . I thought as much. Obviously someone who knew the lie of the land. What I should imagine—'

William never heard what it was the detective would imagine. In fact, he didn't hear very much of anything from that point because the traffic lights changed at the corner of Tettiscombe Road and set in motion a whole long convoy of buses and container lorries. All he could catch were the odd words through the rumble. He heard Gavin saying, '. . . inside job?' and the detective say, 'It could well be, sir; it could well be. The evidence would certainly seem to support that theory.'

Evidence? Did that mean they had found clues? William strained his ears, leaning forward as far as he dared, but all he heard was: '. . . be prepared for the thief to come back. They're very stupid, some of these villains. Never know when enough is enough. Well, I'll be on my way now, sir. You know where we are should you have need of us. I would advise you to keep a sharp look out. Any untoward noises in the night—'

If Alistair and co. could do it, thought William, watching from his hidey-hole as the detective and his constable walked back to their car, there jolly well wasn't any reason why William and co. couldn't!

And who knew? If lead was so valuable, there might even be a reward.

Mash hadn't heard about the tea-leaf. Mash quite often didn't hear of things that went on in the Terrace because unlike Gavin and Mrs Richardson, who were always exchanging gossip as they hung out the washing or emptied the waste-bins, Mrs Khan was shy and didn't talk much. The reason she was shy was that she didn't speak very good English. Mash was trying to teach her, just as William was trying to teach Mash: 'Naffing tea-leaf . . . nicked all the lead.'

'Tea-leaf?' said Mash.

'Tea-leaf,' said William. He leaned forward, speaking very slowly and distinctly. 'Up there—' he pointed. 'Nicking lead. John,' he added.

There was a pause. Mash rolled an agonized eye at Charlotte.

'Means there's a guy called John sitting on the roof making himself a cup of tea,' said Charlotte.

'What does he want to do that for?' said Mash.

'Old English custom,' said Charlotte. She cackled.

William looked at her, crossly. It seemed to him that Charlotte wasn't taking this seriously enough.

'There's bin this geezer,' he said, 'getting up there and stripping all the lead. Stripped it off everyone's place 'cept yours on account of by the time he got to your place he couldn't carry any more, which means he'll most likely be back to c'llect the rest of it either tonight or tomorrer, an' when he does we've got to be ready for him . . . solve the myst'ry before the p'lice do.'

'What mystery?' said Mash.

'Mystery of the tea-leaf,' said William. 'Tea-leaf on the roof. Got to find out who it is. Got to get *organized*—get a campaign going. Look for clues, interview people . . . that kind of thing.'

Mash looked doubtful.

Charlotte said: 'Why can't we go and dig for bodies?'

'We've dug for bodies. We've dug all over and there aren't any. No point keeping on digging for bodies when there isn't any bodies to be dug for.'

'How d'you know there isn't? Could be whole graves full—could be a plague pit. We've only just dug up one little bit.'

'Well, I'm not digging any more,' said William. 'I'm sick of digging. I'm going to catch this tea-leaf and get the reward.'

Charlotte opened her mouth. 'What re—'

'Hands up,' said William, hastily, 'all those that want to help catch the tea-leaf.'

His own hand shot into the air. Geraldine's followed suit.

'She don't even know what a tea-leaf is,' said Charlotte.

'Yes, I do!' said Geraldine.

'No, you don't, and anyway she's too young.'

'That is a very age-ist remark,' said William.

Charlotte tossed her head. 'What if it is, sexist pig!'

She was still nursing a grudge because of what he'd said that morning, about girls not going on roofs.

William put his arm down (it was beginning to ache from being held up), and cleared his throat. Sternly, he said: 'Just because your sister is only seven years old doesn't mean she don't have rights, does it?'

Charlotte scowled. He'd caught her on a weak point—she was always going on about people having rights.

'So what about him?' She jerked her thumb at Mash, sitting cross-legged chewing at his

32

finger. 'He hasn't said what he wants to do yet.'

Guiltily, Mash removed his finger from his mouth.

'I'll do whatever you two are going to do.'

Charlotte raised her eyes heavenwards. 'Oh, brilliant!'

'You gotta vote,' said William. 'Put your hand up if you want to help get the reward.'

Obediently, Mash put his hand up.

'That's three to one,' said William.

'Oh, all *right*.' Charlotte always played fair. 'I'll do it if I have to—but I don't see why we should. P'lice is all pigs. What d'we want to help them for?'

'Get the reward,' said Geraldine.

'*What* re—'

'Thing is,' said William, 'it's not s'much helping them as kind of outwitting them, like . . . finding the tea-leaf before they do.'

Charlotte perked up slightly. 'What, making them look stupid, kind of thing?'

'Yes,' said William. 'Like in Gavin's books.'

'OK!' From her comfortable slouched position on the ground, Charlotte suddenly knelt upright. Her tone was brisk and businesslike. 'If we're going to catch this tea-leaf, then let's *catch* him. What're we just sitting around for? We ought to be out looking for clues and stuff!'

Sometimes William resented it, the way Charlotte just took over.

'There's other things to do first,' he said. 'What we got to do first is make a list.'

'What sort of list?'

'List of suspects.' That was what Alistair and co. always did. 'Then when we've done that, we have to put what their motives could have been, and what opportunity they could have had.'

'Well, then, let's *do* it,' said Charlotte. She sprang to her feet. 'Let's get on with it!'

4

They went up to Charlotte's attic to make their list of suspects. It turned out to be a far more difficult task than William had imagined. Part of the trouble was that they couldn't agree who should go on the list and who shouldn't.

Alistair and co. always started by eliminating people, using what Alistair called 'process of deduction'; but when William suggested using process of deduction to eliminate all the people that lived up in the attics (in other words, Gavin and Sue, Charlotte's parents and Chalky White), Charlotte objected.

She agreed with William that nobody was going to be stupid enough to nick the lead off their own roof and get themselves rained on, but as she pointed out, they didn't actually know for certain that Chalky *had* been rained on. And even if he had, he could cunningly have planned it all beforehand and covered everything in plastic so that it wouldn't get wet.

'He could've nicked the lead off his own roof just to divert suspicion.'

Once they had checked him out, she said, they

could use process of deduction; but until then, she insisted that Chalky be put down as a suspect. Reluctantly, William was forced to agree.

'What about parents?'

'No point putting *them* down.' There was a note almost of scorn in Charlotte's voice. 'Can you see my mum up on the roof? 'Sides, my dad's so straight he blows his top if you just find ten pence in the street . . . tells you it's not yours and you got to put it back again.'

''Course, your dad goes to church,' said William.

'Yeah.' Charlotte pulled a face. It was a sore point with Charlotte, going to church. Going to church meant having to dress up. Charlotte didn't like that.

'My father goes to the mosque,' said Mash.

They knew Mash's father went to the mosque. He went to the mosque on the corner of Station Road and Tettiscombe Grove that had once been a Baptist chapel.

Charlotte picked up her pen. 'Eliminated,' she wrote. 'Mr and Mrs Potter, Mr and Mrs Richardson.'

'Going to the mosque,' said Mash, 'is the same as going to church.'

'Bet it's not as boring,' said Charlotte.

'It's *holy*,' said Mash.

They looked at him. He sounded rather desperate.

'Holy like *church*,' said Mash.

Suddenly, they saw what the problem was—they had eliminated the Potters and the Richardsons, but not the Khans.

'See, ours were rained on,' said Charlotte.

'Mine would've bin if the tea-leaf hadn't had too much to carry,' said Mash.

'But yours don't live in the attics.'

'But they keep things in them!'

'What sort of things?'

Mash put his finger to his mouth. 'Things.'

'Val'ble things?'

Mash chewed at his finger.

'See, if it was val'ble things,' said Charlotte, 'things that were worth a lot of money—'

There was an uncomfortable pause. If it was things that were worth a lot of money, that was a very good reason for Mr Khan not wanting his attics to be rained on. But even if it wasn't things that were worth a lot of money, it still didn't mean that he could be eliminated. They could only eliminate by process of deduction.

William tried explaining this to Mash.

'Wouldn't be scientific otherwise. But I spec' we'll be able to 'liminate him pretty soon. Soon's we start picking up clues. After all, there's lots of other suspects 'sides him.'

'Yeah, like everybody else that lives here,' said Charlotte.

'Dunno 'bout ole Coppins. Can't see him getting up on the roof.'

'He could've had a 'complice.'

'Yes, and he might not be as old as he pretends,' said Mash, eagerly. 'It could be a disguise.'

'And o' course he does live in a scrap heap,' said William. 'F'r all we know he could've tipped

37

off a 'complice to go an' do the nicking, and the lead could be down there, right now, in with all the other stuff.'

Mash was beginning to look happier. He said that he wondered why the police hadn't arrested old man Coppins, or at least got a search warrant for his flat.

''Cos they prob'ly don't know about him living in a scrap heap,' said William. 'That's where we got the advantage . . . we're on the inside.'

'So why don't we tell them?' urged Mash. 'Then they could come and arrest him!'

'Got to have proof first,' said William. 'This is only process of deduction. Anyway, it's us that wants the reward. Don't want the p'lice getting it.'

Mash looked as if he couldn't care one way or the other about the reward just so long as the police came and took old Coppins away so that they could remove Mr Khan's name from the list of suspects.

'What about motive?' said Charlotte. 'What'll I put?'

'Money,' said William.

'"Money",' wrote Charlotte.

It was odd that when Alistair and co. made out lists they were able to uncover all sorts of different motives—*real* motives, like revenge and jealousy and blackmail; but money was the only motive anyone could think of for the inhabitants of Tettiscombe Terrace. It seemed that the entire terrace was in need of it.

The students who lived at number five needed it because they spent all their grant cheques on pot and booze. (They knew they did this because Gavin had said so. Gavin didn't like the students any more than he liked Chalky. He called them drug-sodden hippies and complained about the noise they made and the parties they gave and the mess that they left by the dustbins.) Chalky needed it because he was out of work and living on social security, and Mr Khan needed it because he was saving up to buy a restaurant.

The only person they could think of who didn't seem to need it was the Jogger, and that was annoying, because if anyone was going to be put in prison for being a tea-leaf they would have liked it to be him, even more than old Coppins. Old Coppins, as far as they knew, had never actually done anyone to death, whereas the Jogger was a known killer. They had all witnessed him crushing a snail underfoot, for the sheer malicious pleasure of hearing its shell crack. Furthermore, he had once called the RSPCA to come and murder a stray cat because he said it was spreading fleas (it had been Chalky who had rescued it, taking it off to live with his sister) and only last week he had threatened to 'punch that dog's face in' if Boy didn't stop chasing after him when he jogged.

Charlotte, who hated the Jogger more than anyone, was particularly put out. How could you put someone down as a suspect, she grumbled, if you couldn't think of a motive for them?

'You put my father down,' said Mash.

'Yes, 'cos your father wants money for his restaurant!'

Mash retired in a sulk.

It was William who came up with the suggestion that a person *not* having a motive might also be considered more suspicious than a person having one.

Charlotte brightened up. So did Mash. Mash said that not having a motive sounded to him to be very suspicious indeed. 'Like in your father's books,' he said. 'It's always the person that seems the least likely that turns out to be the one that's done it.'

Mash and Charlotte knew all about Gavin and his books. To William's shame, Gavin insisted on presenting them with copies whenever a new one came out.

'Remember *The Kensington Kidnapping*,' said Charlotte.

'Yes, and the one that all the evidence is against at the beginning turns out to be a red fish,' said Mash.

'Herring,' said William. 'I reckon, if you ask me, there's something we don't know about that Jogger.'

'Like, f'r instance,' said Charlotte, 'where's he get all his money from?'

'Yeah, how come he can afford a new car,' cried Mash, 'when my father can only afford a second-hand one?'

'And ours can't afford one at all,' added Charlotte.

'My father can only afford one because he shares it with my uncle,' said Mash.

'And Chalky got his off a mate,' said William.

'Oh, well! Chalky!' Charlotte tossed her head. 'That old thing of his'll blow up one of these days.'

William was the only person in the terrace who had any feeling for Chalky's Thunderbird—any *good* feeling, that is.

'I s'pose you couldn't expect a girl to understand,' he said.

'Understand what?' screamed Charlotte. 'That it's a stupid old banger that won't go prop'ly?'

'That car goes like a bomb,' said William.

'Yeah . . . like an exploding bomb! Noise it makes!'

'It's meant to make a noise, it's that sort of car. Shows how powerful it is. Do a ton easy, that car will. I bin in it,' said William. 'I bin in it when it's done a ton. Me an' Chalky—'

'Oh, shut up about you and Chalky! Let's get on with things.'

William sat back, muttering. He bet Eliza and Dorothy had never said shut up to Alistair.

'Let's get some paper and make the list out neat so's we can read it,' said Charlotte.

They let Mash write it out because Mash was the best at handwriting. Unfortunately, he wasn't too good at spelling. When he had finished, the list looked like this:

Susspecks	We're they Live	Ther Motiv	There Means + oppertunity	Comments.
Susspeck List Nacher of Crime: Stealing Led of the Roon. Time of Crime: During the night.				
Chorky White	Atticks No. 1	Out of work and needs munny	Through the skylite + has a car for get-a-way	1) Chorky was creem crakered he told wilian he was going to watch the mari crelly + go to bed. 2) wold he take led of his own roof?
AleK marterson (alees the joger)	2nd Flor No. 1.	No noun motiv	Same as above	1) were does he get his munny from?
Students (names not nown)	Ground Flor NO. 5.	Need munny	Same as above but no car for get-a-way	1) students had no respeck for propurty (Gavin say so)
Mr. Khan✱	2nd Fror No. 6	Needs munny for a restorant	Same as above and has a car	1) Mr. Khans roov was the only 1 were the led was not striped 2) Mr. Khan keep things in the atlicks 3) Mr. Khan goes to the mosque.
Mr. Copins	Base-men No. 6	Lives in a scrap heep + led is scrap	Nun nown	1) Mr Copins is probberly too old to clime on the roov 2) He could have had a cumplice.

✱ Ms Richardson thinks Mrs. khan should be a suspeck as well on grounds of sernar quality but no one else das

Then Mash wrote out a list of points to be checked:

1 Did Chorky Wites atick get wet?
2 Were dos the Joger get his munny from?

42

3 Wat dos Mr Khan keep in his atick?
4 Is old Copins really old?
5 Dos old Copins make munny selling his scrap?

Sirtified a true copy
 Sined   Ms Charlotte Richardson
         William Potter
         Mashkoor Khan

on this day 23rd July

They didn't have time to decide who would take charge of which tasks because just as they had finished signing their names Geraldine came thumping up the attic stairs, full of self-righteousness, with a message:

'Charlotte's to come down to tea immediate, else there'll be trouble.'

Mash looked at his watch and discovered it was twenty minutes to six, which meant that Charlotte wasn't the only one for whom there would be trouble. They agreed to meet up again at seven o'clock, 'round by the back steps of number two'. It was by the back steps of number two that the detective had said you could see marks where the tea-leaf had dropped his booty off the roof and dragged it round the side to the getaway vehicle. There were bound to be clues that the police had missed.

Tea for the Potters was scrambled eggs and doorsteps of holy ghost (eggs scrambled by Gavin, doorsteps cut by William) with a large pot of Rosy and some stewed plums. They ate it in the kitchen at six o'clock when Sue came back from work. Sue, naturally, was eager to hear about the roof. William listened carefully as Gavin told her all that the police had said; he was disappointed not to learn any more than he had already discovered for himself. He had thought that Gavin might have had some piece of information that he was keeping up his sleeve, but it seemed the police had found no clues, were not planning to make any arrests, and could only warn residents to keep a sharp look out in case the villain returned.

'They seem to think it's an inside job,' added Gavin. 'My bettings are it's those layabouts at number five . . . either them or Matey at the other end.'

'The White boy? I shouldn't think he'd have the brain.'

'Brain?' Gavin snorted. 'Some brain! Stripping a roof in the middle of a downpour!'

'Yes, that was a bit dim.'

'Dim or vindictive; one or the other.'

At the word vindictive, William came to life. There was only one person he knew who could be described as vindictive.

'Y'know that Jogger,' he said.

'Alec Masterson?' said Sue. 'He gave me a lift in his car this morning. Wasn't that nice?'

Gavin scowled. So did William.

'Heap of tin!' said Gavin.

'I wouldn't say no to it,' said Sue.

William reached out without thinking for the stewed plums. He hated stewed plums more than anything.

'Why don't we get one?'

'Why do you think?' snarled Gavin.

He didn't have to think—he knew.

'Can't afford one.'

'Right! We can't afford one.'

'So how *does* somebody afford one?'

'They sell their soul,' said Gavin, looking hard at Sue. 'Sell their soul to the devil.'

William almost choked on his stewed plums.

'What, you mean the J- Alec Masterson? That's what he's done?'

'Oh, he's sold his all right,' said Gavin. 'Company car, company mortgage . . . he sold his a long time ago!'

After tea, as arranged, they met by the back steps of number two to search for clues. They searched solidly from seven o'clock till bedtime and they didn't find a single one. Not a footprint, not a fingerprint; not even a keyring or a box of matches. They couldn't understand it! Where had all the clues gone? There must have been some. As Alistair had said, in *The Mystery of the Burnt-Out Car*, 'One thing you can be certain of, there's always a clue to be found somewhere. It's just a question of knowing where to look.'

There was nowhere else they *could* look. They had searched every square inch of the flattened area where the lead had been thrown down from the roof. They had even been helped by their own special tracker dog, who had obligingly dug holes every few yards and snuffled into them. At one point the tracker dog had unearthed a bone, which had momentarily excited them, until Charlotte recognized it as one which he had put there himself only a few days ago. It was hardly a very encouraging start to their careers as amateur sleuths.

There was only one bright spot, and that was the knowledge that the Jogger had sold his soul to the devil. As Charlotte said, a person that could do that would be capable of anything.

5

Tap, tap, tap-tap-tap. Tap, tap—

William awoke with a start. What was that? It sounded as if someone was hammering on the wall.

Tap, tap, tap-tap-tap. Tap, tap—

It was Charlotte! She was tapping their emergency signal.

William turned to look at his Mickey Mouse alarm clock. The hands said quarter to twelve.

Quarter to *twelve*? That was the middle of the night!

Tap, tap, tap-tap-tap. Tap, tap—

You couldn't ignore an emergency signal, not even if it was the middle of the night. (Perhaps *especially* not if it were the middle of the night.)

William turned, and with bunched fist rapped out the acknowledgement: tap, tap-tap, tap. Tap, tap-tap, tap. (That meant, I am receiving you, loud and clear, over.)

Thud, went Charlotte, making the wall shake. Thud, bang, *thud*.

That meant she wanted him to meet her downstairs straight away.

Just for a moment, William hesitated; and then he remembered that he was a sleuth, and that it was the bounden duty of a sleuth to go to the aid of fellow sleuths.

Hastily he scrambled out of bed, pulled on his dressing-gown, eased open the attic door and edged through onto the landing.

Down below, all was in darkness; but the moon, shining through the skylight, lit a path ahead of him. He descended the attic stairs sideways, like a crab, taking care not to step on the creaky bits, tiptoed past Gavin and Sue's room, flip-flopped in his slippers down the uncarpeted stairs to the front hall. He had never been out by himself as late as this. It was rather scary.

The front door creaked as he opened it. He didn't have any front door key, so he would just have to put the latch on and hope that nobody crept in under cover of darkness to murder Gavin and Sue in their sleep. Gavin would be furious with him.

He was relieved to see Charlotte already there, crouched in a heap at the bottom of the steps. She put a finger to her mouth, beckoning him to come and crouch with her.

'What is it?' whispered William. 'What's going on?'

'I heard something,' whispered Charlotte. 'Up on the roof. Sounded like someone crashing about . . . I thought it might be the tea-leaf.'

The tea-leaf? 'Good grease!'

'I reckon if we was to sep'rate,' said Charlotte, 'you go down one end, I go down the other, we might stand a chance of catching him.'

William frowned. He wasn't dressed for catching tea-leaves; not in pyjamas and dressing-gown. It was all very well for Charlotte, she'd had time to pull on her sweatshirt and jeans.

'Really,' he said, 'we ought to ring the p'lice.'

'Ring the p'lice? You crazy? Thought you wanted the reward?'

He did, of course; and even more he wanted the honour and glory. *Very well done, you kids! You beat us to it! If it hadn't been for you* . . . but not even Alistair went out catching tea-leaves in his dressing-gown and pyjamas.

'Hang about!' Charlotte suddenly twitched at him. 'Someone's coming.'

They sank back into the shadows. From further down the Terrace they heard the sound of footsteps squelching in the mud; then the tink of keys, and the sound of a car door being opened. William risked a quick look.

'It's Chalky!'

Chalky sprang round. 'Who's that?'

William rose up from his hiding place, followed by Charlotte.

'Oh! It's you, John. Gave me a right fright! What you doin' out at this hour?'

'Thought we heard something,' said William. 'Someone on the roof.'

'What? Someone nicking that naffin lead? I'll have 'em!' cried Chalky. 'You see if I don't!'

Without more ado, Chalky turned and went plunging off across the drive, William and Charlotte close on his heels.

'Where we going?' panted William.

'Goin' up there, John . . . nail the bastard!'

Up the steps of number one they thudded; up the first flight of stairs, up the second, up the third—

'What's that?' said Charlotte. She pointed, distastefully, at a heap of greyish-looking blankets on the floor.

'That's my bed,' said Chalky. 'Having to camp out, ain't I? Got Lupino Laned on.'

William shot a triumphant glance at Charlotte.

'We got Laned on an' all. So'd they.' He jerked a thumb at Charlotte, as they stamped behind Chalky up the attic stairs. 'Gavin says whoever did the job needs his head examined . . . nicking lead in a rainstorm.' (Lupino Lanestorm?) 'Gavin says they must be a raving nutter.'

'Oh, he does, does he?' From one of the attics, Chalky had dragged an old rickety table and was positioning it beneath the skylight. 'What does Gavin use for weather forecasting?' He swung himself up onto the table. 'Bit of seaweed?'

'Listens to the radio,' said William, puzzled.

'Yeah? So that's what the tea-leaf prob'ly done . . . listened to the naffin' radio, what got it naffin' wrong. Now, you just keep stumm, you two. Don't want to scare him off.'

Carefully, Chalky eased open the skylight. Slowly, like someone emerging from the conning tower of a submarine, he poked his head up.

'Anything there?' whispered Charlotte.

'Not's far as I can see. But I think we'll just have a quick gander.'

'Can we have a quick gander, too?' said Charlotte.

'You wanna come onna roof?' Amiably, Chalky reached down a hand. 'All right, then . . . let's be having yer!'

Charlotte, William was annoyed to note, scrambled up quite easily. When it came to his turn his dressing-gown got in the way and wrapped itself round his head and tried to throttle him. By the time he had fought his way free, Charlotte had already gone rushing ahead in her zest to explore.

'Looking for clues,' she said, afterwards.

Just showing off, if you asked him. He really was beginning to wonder about these noises she was supposed to have heard. She kept darting off in all directions, prancing about near the edge in a way that made William feel quite ill. It also made him feel inferior. It had never occurred to him that Charlotte might have a head for heights and that he might not. It was all wrong! In Gavin's books it was always Alistair who did things, not the girls.

They tramped all the way down from one end of the roof to the other. If anybody had been there, they certainly weren't there now.

'I reckon it must have bin them naffin' birds,' said Chalky. 'Clump about like they've got hob-nailed boots, some o' them things.'

Charlotte agreed; but in spite of deciding it was birds, both she and Chalky were eager to check that the lead was still in place on the attics of number six.

'Tea-leaf could have got away with it before we got up here,' said Charlotte; and Chalky said don't you worry, he'd nail the bastard.

Happily there wasn't any need, for the lead was still there, stretched out all grey and flat (not looking in the least bit like bed sheets).

'That's OK, then,' said Chalky. He knelt, and patted it. 'Had me worried for a minute ... thought of some tea-leaf coming here nicking what don't b'long to him.'

'Thought that was what tea-leaves always did,' said Charlotte.

'Yeah, well, what I mean,' said Chalky, 'what I mean, someone from outside, like ... coming here doin' his nicking.'

Back downstairs Chalky told them to 'Nip along, now, smartish ... kids your age, you shouldn't be out this time o'night. Give me quite a turn, seeing you come up at me.'

'Were you going somewhere?' said Charlotte.

('I had to ask,' she said later, when William accused her of treating Chalky as if he were still a suspect. 'We're s'posed to be sleuthing, aren't we?')

Chalky said he'd just popped down to put the old jam jar to bed: 'Check I locked her up ... can't be too careful, with all these naffin' tea-leaves about.'

William nodded and said, 'That's right. Vintage jam jar like that, be one of the first things they'd nick.'

As they made their way back along the drive to their own houses a dark figure suddenly loomed up in front of them. Charlotte gave a little breathy squeak and clutched at William's arm, but it was only the Jogger, coming back from his jogging.

'Funny time o' night to be at it,' said William, when they were discussing it later. 'Who goes jogging in the middle o' the night?'

'Yeah, unless they're up to no good,' said Mash.

It was another damning piece of evidence against the Jogger: 1) he had sold his soul to the devil, 2) he went jogging in the middle of the night.

William, just to be polite, and because he knew that it annoyed him, said, 'Evening, Mr Masterson.'

The Jogger, in reply, turned his head and hissed. He looked as if he would like to wring their necks. If it hadn't been for Chalky, putting his jam jar to bed, William had the feeling that he would have murdered them there and then and buried their bodies in the back garden. Even Charlotte agreed that his behaviour had been suspicious.

'Obviously didn't want to be seen. Didn't like it one little bit when he bumped into us.'

Charlotte hadn't liked it one little bit, either. William fell asleep savouring the fact that she had squeaked and clutched his arm. It made up for the butch way she had behaved on the roof.

Next morning, as she flew about the kitchen snatching at her breakfast, Sue said, 'Well! Fancy you missing out on all the excitement.'

William looked at her, guardedly. 'What excitement?'

'Last night,' said Sue. 'Our friendly neighbourhood tea-leaf put in another appearance.'

'Oh, that!' said William. 'That was just pigeons, that was . . . pigeons on the roof.'

'How do you know?' said Sue. 'You were fast asleep! I came up afterwards and checked. Anyway, it wasn't pigeons . . . not unless you think that pigeons are capable of rolling up hefty great chunks of lead.'

William stopped, in the act of shaking out cornflakes.

'Who says it was rolled up?' It certainly hadn't been rolled up when he had seen it.

'The police,' said Sue.

'P'lice?'

'Yes, you know . . . the ones in blue, with the helmets.'

William scowled. He could do without the sarcasm. This was serious.

'What was the p'lice doing here?'

'Mr Richardson called them. He heard a noise and dialled 999 and they sent someone round.'

'What, and they caught someone?' William asked anxiously. He didn't understand what was going on here—after all, he had been on the roof: he had *seen*—but if the police had gone and caught someone, that would be an end of it. To his relief, Sue shook her head.

'No, unfortunately they arrived just a bit too late. But they obviously disturbed him, because he had to leave all the lead behind.'

That was all right, then. William went back to his cornflakes.

'S'what time ws it? When the p'lice came?'

'Oh, I don't know . . . about half-past one, I should think. In fact it was, exactly; I remember looking at the clock, and wondering what on earth was going on. I thought a war had started . . . car doors slamming, people running about . . . the most frightful racket! Imagine you sleeping through it.'

'Yes—imagine! Would that we might all have been so lucky.' Gavin had appeared at the kitchen door. He was still wearing his dressing-gown and pyjamas, with his chin all bristly and his hair sticking on end, eyes blinking irritably without their glasses. 'For your information, I have had precisely three hours and twenty-two minutes of uninterrupted sleep!'

'That's because you would insist on going downstairs to have a look. And then he got over-excited,' said Sue, 'and spent the rest of the night talking.'

'I should think I did get over-excited! People tramping about all over the roof half the night . . . dear God!' Gavin clamped a hand to his forehead. 'Where is it all going to end?'

'Stop being so melodramatic,' said Sue. 'We shall be re-housed in a week or two, then they can tramp about as much as they like.'

'Yes! And what happens in the meantime?' Gavin glowered at her, screwing up his eyes in an effort to see. 'Before we know it they'll be swarming through the skylight helping themselves to just whatever they fancy!'

'If they can find anything worth helping themselves to in this place,' said Sue, 'they're welcome.'

'My manuscript,' said Gavin. He flung out an arm. 'My manuscript!'

'Sleep with it under your pillow. William, I'm off. If you want any ghost—'

'I'll do it myself.'

'That's a boy!'

Sue patted his head as she whirled past. They heard her clattering down the stairs.

'Half-past one inna morning.' William pondered it as he spooned sugar over his cornflakes. It had been midnight when they had caught the Jogger creeping along in the darkness. He bet it was the Jogger whom Charlotte had heard on the roof.

What must have happened, he must have been up there all the time. He must have seen the skylight opening and immediately dived out of sight behind one of the chimney stacks. Then he would have waited till Chalky and the others had gone back down, slipped in after them, nipped out through the back and gone racing round the block pretending to be doing his jogging.

The more William thought about it, the more likely it seemed. He had obviously gone back indoors for an hour, waited till he thought the coast was clear, then crept back out again to get on with his tea-leafing—only to be interrupted for a second time by Mr Richardson calling the police.

'S'what's happened to the stuff?' said William.

'Eh?' Gavin was busy huffing and puffing on the lenses of his spectacles. 'What stuff?'

'Stuff he was trying to nick.'

'If you're referring to the lead—' huff—'it's been left where it is. All nicely rolled up—' huff— 'waiting for him to come back and get it.'

William stared. They were going to let him *get* it?

'It's what is known as bait,' said Gavin. Having huffed to his satisfaction he picked up the corner of the tablecloth and began polishing with it. 'An open invitation.'

'What, they're going to do a stake-out?' It was what they had done in *The Mystery of the Kensington Kidnapping*. That had been one of the more exciting ones. The only trouble was, if the police were going to set up listening posts, with bugging devices and—

The police, said Gavin, were not going to set up listening posts with bugging devices. Not in Tettiscombe Terrace. Not for a mere tea-leaf.

Gavin sounded rather sour about it. He said that the few remaining inhabitants of the Terrace were being left like sacrificial lambs, just waiting to be burgled.

'"Cept I shouldn't think the tea-leaf'd risk coming back a third time,' said William, wistfully.

'Well, I'm not taking any chances!' Gavin rammed his spectacles onto his nose. 'If the law won't protect us, we shall have to protect ourselves.'

William looked at him, alarmed. He didn't want Gavin interfering! Sue was all right, she wasn't any bother; but if Gavin were going to start poking his nose in—

William pushed back his chair with a clatter. He would have to do without any ghost this morning. If Gavin were going to start poking his nose in, there wasn't a moment to lose.

'Where are you off to?' roared Gavin.

'Going out,' said William. 'Got things to do.'

'Yes,' said Gavin, 'and so have I! It may have escaped your attention that I have a book to write. I can't be expected to cope with all the shopping and the housework and the—'

William fled.

6

On his way down the steps, William bumped into Charlotte on her way up.

'Hey!' said Charlotte. 'D'you hear what happened?'

'Yes,' said William.

'He came back! Last night! My dad got the p'lice!'

'I know,' said William. 'Gavin told me.'

'They went up through our skylight . . . came up the stairs and stood on a table. Two of them, there were. A big one and a little one. I talked to them,' said Charlotte. 'I had this long conversation. I told them about our attics getting wet. I told them—'

'Hope you didn't tell them about us?'

''Course I didn't tell them about us! What d'you take me for? 'n idiot?' Charlotte looked at him, indignantly. 'We want to get the reward, don't we?'

'Well, if we do,' said William, 'we'd better jolly well get a move on, 'fore Gavin starts interfering. I don't reckon we got much time. You get Geraldine an' I'll get Mash . . . see you round the back.'

Mash, as usual, hadn't heard anything of the events that had taken place during the night. He became very excited when he learnt that the tea-leaf had been back and had stripped the remaining lead off the roof.

'That means if it rains my father's attic will get wet!'

'*If* it rains,' said Charlotte. 'It hasn't yet.'

Mash peered up at the sky. 'It might,' he said, hopefully.

It did look quite grey and threatening.

'If it starts to rain we'll let it go on a bit, then you can go back indoors and find out what's happened . . . see if it's come in and ruined things,' said Charlotte.

'And see what those things are,' said William.

'Yeah, see if they're val'ble.'

'And if they are,' said Mash, eagerly, 'then we can use process of deduction?'

They agreed that then they could use process of deduction; but in the meantime, said Charlotte, while they were waiting for it to start raining, they ought to organize another search for clues.

'After all, we know the tea-leaf was here last night, and he might just've left something.'

They did a circuit round the Terrace, walking very slowly with their heads down. Boy walked with them; his head was down, too. Charlotte said that he was looking for clues and that they must go where he led them, because dogs had an instinct for these things. William was privately doubtful—in his experience, the only thing Boy had an instinct for was food— but Charlotte insisted that if there was anything to be found, Boy would find it.

After he'd dragged them three times round the dustbins ('We got to follow him,' said Charlotte, 'he knows what he's doing.') even Mash began to wonder out loud whether he might be not so much a tracking sort of dog as an eating sort of dog; a suggestion which Charlotte treated with contempt.

'All dogs is eating sort of dogs ... couldn't stay alive if they didn't eat, could they? There's a good boy! Find something! Find!'

Eagerly, Boy stood on his hind legs and tipped the lid off the nearest dustbin. Inside was a Kentucky fried chicken box containing a load of old chicken bones, the remains of someone's Chinese meal, and a piece of scrumpled-up rag. Boy dived triumphantly on the chicken bones. While Charlotte was wresting them from him, William, using a bit of twig torn from the yew hedge ('never touch possible clues with the bare hand'), fished out the rag. It was bloodstained.

Bloodstained.

He'd found a bloodstained rag!

William waved it exultantly on the end of his twig.

'Look what I've got!'

They looked.

'I told you he had an instinct,' said Charlotte.

Mash, who tended to be squeamish, recoiled as the rag brushed his nose. 'What is it?'

'Clue!' said William. 'Clue to who done it!'

Bloodstained rags always were. Alistair and co. had once discovered one stuffed in the hollow of a blasted oak and it had led them straight to the guilty party.

'I suppose what must have happened,' said Charlotte, 'he must have cut his finger, folding up the lead—'

'Wasn't a finger,' said Geraldine. She hadn't been very much use up until now, being more interested in turning cartwheels and walking about on her hands than in looking for clues. 'It was his nose.'

There was a pause.

'Whose nose?' said Charlotte.

'That Jogger person's.'

They stared at her, astounded.

'How d'you know?'

'Seen him,' said Geraldine. 'Yesterday, when you was all upstairs writing things . . . he come home from work in his car and he gets out and tries to open the boot and it won't open, so then he sees me watching him and he shouts "What do you want? Go away!" and just as he's doing that the boot flies up and bonks him on the nose and he shouts "Damn and blars! Now look what you've made me do!" and he pulls out this bit of rag and bleeds into it. Then he goes and puts it in the dustbin.'

There was a silence. William struggled between glee at the thought of the Jogger being bonked on the nose by a flying car boot (and shouting damn and blars) and regret that the bloodstained rag couldn't be regarded as a clue any more.

Charlotte was the first to rally.

'What we got to ask ourselves is, why was he opening his boot in the first place?'

'That's right,' Mash nodded. 'What had he got in there?'

'Obviously something he didn't want people to see.'

'Yeah, otherwise why should he shout at her?'

Charlotte suddenly snatched at the rag and thrust it under Boy's nose. 'Smell!' she commanded.

Boy snuffled, obligingly. His mouth opened.

'Watch it!' yelled William. 'He's going to eat it!'

Whoever heard of a clue being devoured by a dog?

'Good boy!' said Charlotte. 'Leave!' She wrenched the remains of the rag out of Boy's jaws. 'Now, seek!' she said. 'Find!'

Boy looked up at her, grinning amiably and chewing on his bit of rag.

'Find!' said Charlotte. She pointed dramatically into the air. 'Follow!'

Boy put his head on one side. Slowly his tail moved back and forth. He was plainly willing to oblige but couldn't quite work out what was wanted of him.

'*GO!*' roared Charlotte.

Boy went. Charlotte went with him, flat out at the end of his lead, William and Mash galloping after, Geraldine trailing in the rear. Down the drive they galloped, round the side of the houses, across the back gardens, plunging over walls, tumbling into ditches, following the trail of the tracker dog through hedges of bramble and thickets of thistle and thorn.

Scraped, slashed, stabbed and stung, they came at last to a breathless halt.

'This is where we were yesterday!' panted Mash.

Boy had brought them straight back to the scene of the crime—to the steps of number two, where the tea-leaf had deposited his booty before dragging it round to the getaway vehicle.

'This is no good!' said William. 'We've already bin over all this!'

'Just have to go over it again, then. He wouldn't have brought us here for nothing. He's not stupid.' Charlotte was busy letting Boy off his lead. 'Must be something we missed . . . Find! Good boy! Find!'

'We went over every inch!' grumbled Mash.

'Follow him!' roared Charlotte.

Boy was questing to and fro, excitedly, nose to ground, tail flattened. Single file, crouched low like Indian braves, they crept in circles after him. First they crept this way, then they crept that way. Every time Boy made a sudden turn, they all crashed into each other. After having been squashed once and flattened twice (being the smallest, she was at the end of the line) Geraldine declared that she was tired of this game and wanted to play something else.

Suddenly there was a shriek from Charlotte: 'Look!'

'What?'

They tumbled about her in their eagerness to see. Charlotte pointed: 'A footprint!'

A footprint!

Awestruck, they gathered round. There it was, an actual footprint . . . lying there, large as life, in the mud.

'Wasn't there yesterday,' said Mash. 'We'd have noticed it.'

'Must've bin left there in the night.'

'Left there by the leaf!' Mash bent down excitedly. 'This is the leaf's footprint! We've got his footprint! That means we can call the p'lice, we can have him arrested!'

William frowned. It wasn't as easy as that. He knew about footprints. Alistair and co. had once discovered one in *The Mystery of the One-Legged Man*. You couldn't just jump to conclusions, you had to be scientific about it. You had to take measurements, and do drawings, and make a plaster cast, and then you had to go round checking and comparing.

'Just 'cos we got the footprint,' he said, 'doesn't mean to say we know who it b'longs to.'

Mash stared at him. 'B'longs to the Jogger! We followed the trail!'

'Boy followed the trail,' said Charlotte. 'We just followed Boy.'

William looked at Boy. He had now located the bone which he had unearthed yesterday and was happily settling down to gnaw at it. William had a funny kind of feeling that it was the bone he had been trailing all along.

He cleared his throat. One had to be stern. Alistair was stern.

'Thing is,' said William, 'finding a footprint's just a start . . . what we got to do now is establish things.'

'What sort of things?' Mash was down on his hands and knees, poring over the print.

'Like, what kind of shoe it was, and what size, and what make, and all that . . . we've not got to get carried away,' said William. 'We got to have proof.'

Mash looked as if he might be going to argue; support, unexpectedly, came from Charlotte. (She, too, had just noticed Boy, gnawing on his bone.)

'He's right. If you don't have proof, you haven't got a case.'

'So how d'you get it?' said Mash, sullenly. 'How d'you get this proof?'

'First you measure,' said William. 'Somebody go and get a ruler and a pencil and a bit of paper.'

He waited. They stood, looking at him.

'All right,' said William. 'We'll *all* go . . . I'll get the ruler, and Charlotte can get the paper and pencil, and you can get some flour off of your mother.'

'Flour?' Mash looked mystified. 'What do we want that for?'

Mash hadn't read *The Mystery of the One-Legged Man*—it had been written before he came to the Terrace.

'Flour and water,' said William. 'Make a cast. Get the shape of it.'

Mash shook his head. He plainly didn't think much of the idea.

They left Geraldine guarding the footprint, with strict instructions not to allow anybody near it.

'And if *he* appears, set Boy on him.'

Indoors, William found Gavin wrestling up the stairs with a huge plank of wood. The plank of wood looked vaguely familiar (he recognized it later as the door from a cupboard down in the basement).

'Good!' said Gavin. 'Now that you're back—'

'Can't stop,' said William. 'Got things to do!'

Gavin said that so had he. *He* was busy protecting house and home. He was going to nail the plank of wood over the skylight so that people couldn't come swarming in at dead of night and murdering them all in their beds. So if William could very kindly stop messing about at whatever it was he was messing about at—

'Can't hear you!' shouted William.

He grabbed his ruler and ran, leaving Gavin swearing on the stairs.

When they got back to number two, they found that Boy was sitting on the footprint. Geraldine, nearby, was squatting on her haunches, quietly humming to herself as she plaited bits of greenery.

'What's all this?' cried William.

Geraldine, totally unconcerned, began to arrange the bits of greenery in her hair.

'It's all right, he's guarding it.'

'*Guarding* it?' William looked indignantly at Boy, sitting on the footprint. 'Squashing it flat, more like!'

Mash, in a fury, rushed at Boy, waving his plastic bag full of flour.

'Get him off, get him off! There won't be any of it left!'

Some of it was left; but by no means all. Mostly it was an impression of Boy's rear end, with just the front part of a shoe sticking out of it.

'This is a bit plum duff!' William regarded Geraldine accusingly. 'Now we've only got half a footprint!'

'You don't have to go on at her,' said Charlotte. Charlotte could go on at her, but nobody else could. 'She's only seven. She don't know any better.'

Spickanspan was only seven, but *he* knew better. Spickanspan would never let a clue get ruined by being sat on.

'Anyway, it's not as bad as all that.' Charlotte was down on her knees, examining it. 'You can see how long it was, more or less—you can tell what sort of shoe it was.'

'A jogging shoe,' said Mash.

'Let's get and start measuring.' William moved in, with his ruler. It was about time he took command. 'Let's get it measured before somebody goes an' walks on it.'

As far as they could make out, the shoe measured about twenty-eight centimetres from one end to the other (from the end that they could see to the end that had been obliterated by Boy's bum print). The front half measured ten centimetres from side to side at the widest part. The pattern on it (drawn by Mash) looked like this:

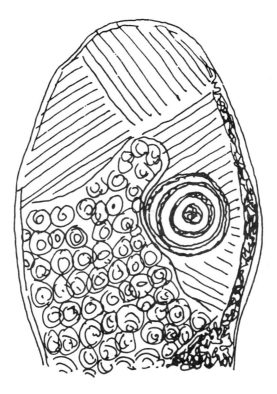

The flour-and-water cast didn't look like anything at all. They mixed the flour and water to a pulp and pressed it down most carefully, just as Alistair had done in *The Mystery of the One-Legged Man*, and they left it for ten minutes to harden, which was what Alistair had said you should do. But when they tried to peel it off again it just stuck to their hands in nasty cloggy lumps. Lots of it stuck to the footprint, as well, and got so thoroughly churned up with the earth that it was impossible to remove it. In the end, instead of having half a footprint and one bum print, they just had a mess of greyish sludge. It was most frustrating—Alistair and co. had been able to take theirs home and put it in the oven and bake it.

William speculated that possibly it had something to do with Alistair's footprint having been found on the beach, in nice firm sand, whereas theirs had been found in common-or-garden ordinary earth.

Charlotte wondered if perhaps the flour that Mrs Khan used for making her chapattis might be the wrong sort of flour for making plaster casts. Perhaps they should have used self-raising flour.

Mash said that there wasn't anything wrong with the flour, chapatti sort of flour was just as good as any other sort of flour, it was the fact that they had made the mixture too wet; to which Charlotte, who was the one who had actually done the mixing, angrily retorted that it hadn't been too wet at all, it had started off just right.

'What we ought to've done, we ought to've held a numbrella over it, stop it getting sloshy.'

It was only then that they realized—it had been raining steadily for the last half hour. . .

7

The rain dripped dismally throughout lunch. Gavin, threatening vengeance on all and sundry if his study should have so much as a dribble descend upon it, went chasing up the attic stairs to check, but the Council had covered the roof with roofing felt and Gavin's attic was as dry as a bone.

Gavin said, 'Hm! Just as well!' and stumped back down the stairs.

'If you're going to be in this afternoon,' he said to William, 'you can help me with the next bit of my plot . . . I want to see if it would be possible for Eliza to get her hand through the letter box and open the front door without a key.'

William looked at him, darkly. The last time he had helped Gavin with a plot he had ended up stuck inside a chimney pot.

'I got things to do,' he said.

'But I can't get on with my chapter until I've found out. I insist—' Gavin thumped the table with his fist— 'I insist that you come and put your hand through the letter box!'

'I'll do it later. Can't stop now. Got a meeting.'

William snatched up an apple and ran.

On wet days the gang met under a chestnut tree at the foot of the garden to number two. It was dry under there, and there were bits of log and an upturned bucket to sit on. William perched himself on the bucket and munched at his apple as he waited for the others. They all arrived together, Charlotte, Geraldine and Boy, with Mash capering ahead of them, shouting. As they drew near, William was able to make out the words:

'My father's attic has been rained on! Everything has been ruined!'

He sounded triumphant.

'So what was in there?' said William.

Mash beamed. 'Suitcases,' he said.

'*Suitcases?*'

'All the suitcases we used when we came to England. And now they've all been rained on. My mother is very upset.'

They looked at him, blankly.

'What did they have in them?' said Charlotte. 'Gold, or something?'

'Clothes,' said Mash. 'All our clothes that we can't keep elsewhere. This is why—' he lowered his voice— 'this is why nobody must know.'

'Why?'

'Because of the Council. If they discovered that we were keeping things up there—'

There was a silence.

'What?' said Charlotte.

'They would make us pay more rent.'

Mr Khan couldn't afford to pay more rent—he was saving up every penny to buy his restauant.

'This is why—' Mash looked at them, earnestly— 'you mustn't ever tell.'

'Who's likely to?' The last thing Charlotte would ever do was tell. She jerked her head. 'Let's get on with things!'

From out of the back pocket of her jeans she pulled a pencil and the list of suspects (a trifle crumpled, from having been sat on).

'"Points to be checked,"' read Charlotte. '"No. 1, did Chalky's attics get rained on?" Yes. So he can be eliminated.' She ticked point no. 1 and drew a line through Chalky's name. '"Point no. 2, where does the Jogger get his money from?"'

'Sells his soul,' said William.

Charlotte hesitated. 'What's it mean? Exackly?'

'Means he works in a bank.'

'Works in a bank,' wrote Charlotte. '"No. 3, what does Mr Khan keep in his attic?" Answer: suitcases.'

'Which have all got rained on,' prompted Mash.

'Which have all got rained on,' repeated Charlotte as she wrote it down.

'So now he can be eliminated, too.'

Charlotte looked at William.

'I s'pose so,' said William. He still didn't really see that suitcases could be classed as valuable, or why anyone should particularly care if they got rained on, but Mr Khan obviously wasn't the tea-leaf, they all knew who the tea-leaf was. Mr Khan had simply been a red herring.

'That just leaves ole Coppins.' Charlotte sat upright on her log. '"Is ole Coppins really old? Does ole Coppins make money selling scrap?"'

'Dunno how we're going to find that out,' said William. It seemed a bit pointless, now. They *knew* who the tea-leaf was, they'd practically caught him at it.

It was Charlotte who reminded him that they ought not to jump to conclusions.

'We've still got to check people's footprints. And what about them students?'

They had forgotten about the students. They still didn't even know their names. Mash said, 'Why don't we go and ask them?' but of course that wasn't the way that things were done. You didn't just go up to a suspect and say, 'What are you called?' It would be far too obvious.

'They'd know at once that you was on to them.'

'"Sides, we're meant to be detectives,' said William. 'Finding things out.'

'Best make another list,' said Charlotte. '"Things to be Done."'

Charlotte's list read like this:

THINGS TO BE DONE
1) Find out about old Coppins
2) Find out about the students
3) Check footprints of a) Jogger
                                    b) Old Coppins
                                    c) Students

Mash said he didn't see why they had to do all that. He didn't see why they couldn't just check the Jogger. 'Then if the footprint's his, that's proof it's him.'

Charlotte disagreed. She said for all they knew there could be more than one person walking round with the same foot size and the same pattern on their shoes. She said the only way they could eliminate old man Coppins and the students was by checking them out.

'What we've got to decide is who's going to do what.'

Mash said that he would find out the names of the students—he said he had thought of a way of doing it without having to ask them. William volunteered to collect footprints. That left Charlotte with old man Coppins.

There was a pause.

'It's prob'ly best for you to do it,' said William. 'Being a girl.'

Old man Coppins was less likely to be nasty to a girl. If Mash or William approached him, he could turn violent.

Charlotte tossed her head.

'Needn't think I'm scared of him!'

'I'm not *scared* of him,' said William.

Mash said neither was he, but he had to think of his mother—it could be dangerous for her, being in the same house.

Charlotte didn't say anything; she just looked at them both and gave a little contemptuous smile.

What they had to decide next was how they were going to get people's footprints. It had been easy for Alistair in *The Mystery of the One-Legged Man,* because at some time or another every single one of his suspects had obligingly gone for a stroll along the beach and left a perfect set of prints in the sand. William and co. were going to have to think of something else. Mash came up with the bright idea of using a pot of black gunge which had been left behind by the Council workmen after their repairs to the roof. They could lay a trail of it, he said, and wait for people to walk in it.

They all trooped off to inspect the black gunge, but it had turned solid overnight. There was half a tin of red paint in a shed at the bottom of one of the gardens, but as Charlotte pointed out, no one was very likely to go round putting their feet in a trail of red paint. Black gunge mightn't have been noticed; but you could hardly miss red paint.

'What we really need,' said William, 'is sand.'

Unexpectedly, because nobody thought she had been paying attention, Geraldine said that she knew where there was sand; lots and lots of sand.

'Where?' said William.

'Brighton beach,' said Charlotte, and cackled.

'Up the road,' said Geraldine. 'That place where they're making all the houses.'

She meant the building site at the corner of Tettiscombe Grove.

'There's men working there,' said Mash. 'They'll get mad if we steal their sand.'

Geraldine said no they wouldn't, she'd been there the other day and filled up all her dolls' pram with it.

'What d'you go and do that for?' said Charlotte.

Geraldine said she was going to make a beach, and build sand castles, only she hadn't got around to it yet, so the sand was still there, in the dolls' pram (along with the dolls).

After some rather bitter bargaining—Geraldine didn't seem to appreciate that they needed the sand for more important purposes than simply building sand castles—she agreed that they could 'borrow' some of it, on condition they either returned it afterwards or got her some more.

'We'll get you some more,' said William; and he humped the pram quickly down the front steps before Geraldine could change her mind.

Charlotte, who had gone back indoors, now reappeared with a bright red frying pan which she proceeded to fill from the dolls' pram.

'What's that for?' said William.

Charlotte said it was for two things. Firstly it was to carry sand down to old man Coppins's basement so that they could scatter it on the ground and get his footprint; and second, when the sand had been emptied out, it was to offer to old man Coppins as scrap and see if he wanted to buy it.

'See, this is a really good frying pan . . . it was my dad's birthday present to my mum. She doesn't know I've got it. She'd do her nut if she knew I'd got it. But I reckon if ole Coppins is really into making money he'll try and buy it off of us . . . course, I won't let him. I'll say I've changed my mind or he ain't offered enough. My mum'd go spare if I went and sold her best frying pan.'

Charlotte with her frying pan, with Geraldine and Boy, set off up the drive to old man Coppins.

William and Mash, pushing the pram, trundled off to number five. There, while William set about sprinkling sand at the foot of the steps, Mash went up to the front door to examine the array of bells and see if by any chance the names of the students were there. A few seconds later he came bouncing back down, looking jubilant.

'Did you find them?' said William.

Mash said yes, he had found them—one was called Prole, and the other was Druggie. They seemed rather strange sort of names. William wondered for a minute whether they could be false, except that there was a girl at school called Josephine Smellie, and he supposed if people could be called Smellie then they could be called almost anything. Anyway, said Mash, Prole and Druggie was what it said by the side of the bells.

William had almost but not quite finished sprinkling his sand, with Mash kneeling down helping to spread it smooth, when two dark shapes loomed up behind them and a deep voice said, 'Hallo, 'allo, 'allo! What have we here?'

William jumped. Mash scrambled in a panic to his feet. The law!

It wasn't the law, it was the students. But as William said afterwards, it was still a nasty moment. You never knew when people were going to turn violent.

The students didn't actually look violent. One of them, the one who had pretended to be the law, was short and rather plump, with wispy red hair and a straggly beard. The other was thin and weedy with a long neck and lots of pimples.

'What you up to, then?' said the bearded one. He didn't sound unfriendly; just curious.

William sat back, rather sternly, on his heels.

'We're spreading sand,' he said. As he explained to Charlotte, later, they could see that he was spreading sand, he had a whole pramful of it, so really there wasn't very much point in saying he was prospecting for gold or looking for bodies, which were the only other things that immediately occurred to him.

'That's a useful thing to do,' said the Beard. 'Spreading sand . . . I wonder more people don't take that up.'

'Are we allowed to tread on it?' asked Pimples.

'Yes,' said William. 'We want people to tread on it. The more people that tread on it, the more it'll help smash it down.'

'Oh, well! In that case—' Pimples set a large plimsolled foot on top of the sand. 'There you go! That should do the trick!'

'What happens when it's been smashed?' said the Beard, obligingly trampling up and down. 'Are you going to build something on it? A cathedral, or something?'

'We haven't decided yet,' said William. He bent over the footprints. 'You are Mr Prole and Mr Druggie?' he said.

They looked at each other. 'I suppose we must be,' said Pimples.

'Are you or aren't you?' said William. He needed to know, so that he could make a proper report on the footprints. Footprints weren't any use if you couldn't say for certain who they belonged to. 'Which one of you is Mr Prole?'

They pointed. 'I'm Prole—'

'He's Prole—'

'And I'm Druggie.'

'He's Druggie.'

It seemed that Prole was the pimply one. Prole's footprint was immensely long and narrow. William couldn't very well take out his ruler and measure it in front of them, but it looked as if it must be at least thirty centimetres. Druggie was the one with the beard. Druggie's footprint was short and squat. It looked as if it measured almost as much widthways as it did lengthways. More like a dinner plate than a footprint.

Prole and Druggie went up the steps and disappeared indoors. Something seemed to have amused them, because they were laughing. William didn't have the time to waste wondering what it was. Just as he had suspected, Prole's footprint was far too long, Druggie's far too short.

'They're no good, then,' said Mash. 'That's them wiped out.'

Unless of course one of them was wearing false shoes—but no, it didn't seem likely.

'Better make a note of it,' said William. 'Prole and Druggie ... bin eliminated.' He looked at Mash. 'You sure they're called Prole and Druggie?'

'It's what it says on the door,' said Mash.

It wasn't what it said on the door at all. What it said on the door, quite clearly—well, reasonably clearly—well, if you weren't an idiot—was Paul and Duggie.

'How was I to know?' said Mash, sulking. 'I've never heard of anyone called Duggie.'

They walked back down the drive, arguing hotly as they went.

'Bet you've never heard of anyone called Jahangir!'

'Bet that's not as common as Duggie.'

'Bet it is!'

'Bet it isn't!'

'Bet there's about a million people called that in Bangladesh.'

'Bet there isn't even one in England!'

Just in time, in the middle of the argument, William remembered to stop outside the steps of the Jogger's house and scatter some more sand from his dolls' pram ready for the Jogger to step in when he came home from work.

Back at the chestnut tree they found Charlotte sharing a big bag of chips with Geraldine and Boy.

'Hey!' shouted William. 'Where d'you get them from?'

'Chippie over the road.'

'Thought you were s'posed to be going down to ole Coppins?'

'Went there.'

'S'what happened?' William settled himself on the log beside her. 'Let's have one!'

'No,' said Charlotte. 'Only people that go on dangerous missions get to eat chips.' She held out the bag to Boy, who helped himself to a large mouthful. She wouldn't let Mash or William get near enough even to sniff.

'Was it very terrible?' said Mash.

'Awful.' Charlotte crammed her mouth with chips. 'Reckon we was lucky to escape with our lives.'

'Ours was pretty dangerous,' said William. 'Taking footprints—'

Charlotte looked at him.

'What's he like?' said Mash. 'Is he a vampire?'

'Shouldn't be surprised.'

'Has he got fangs?'

'Yeah . . . great huge things, covered in blood.'

Mash gulped.

'I like Mr Coppins,' said Geraldine. 'He's nice. He felt sorry for us. He said anyone what's got to go round selling their mum's best frying pan's got to be really starving, and he said was I really starving, and I said yes, 'cos I was, 'cos it was greens for dinner and I didn't eat any, and so he give us twenty pence for some chips an'—'

'An' he's really dangerous?' said William.

'He could've bin,' said Charlotte.

'Well, o'course, he could've bin, but I'd've gone instead then, wouldn't I? Don't think I'd've let you go if I'd really thought he was dangerous, do you? What d'you take me for?'

'A pig!' screeched Charlotte. She screwed up her chip paper and hurled it at him. '"*Don't think I'd've let you go*" . . . I'd like to see you try 'n stop me!'

William picked up the chip paper and dropped it disdainfully to the ground.

'When you have quite finished shouting abuse at me,' he said (it was what Alistair had said to Dorothy, when in a rare moment of rebellion she had called him a foul domineering beast),

'I think we ought to see what we've managed to 'stablish.'

'Make a list,' urged Mash.

The list read like this:

THINGS THAT HAVE BEEN ESTABLISHED

1) Old Coppins is old (probably about 86)
2) His feet are a funny shape (with nobbles)
3) He does not buy frying pans to sell as scrap
4) The students are called Paul and Duggie
5) Paul's feet are too small
6) Duggie's feet are too large
7) This means we can eliminate
    a) Old Coppins
    b) the Students
8) This means there is only one suspect left and that is the Jogger

Mash wanted them to put a number 9—This means the Jogger is the tea-leaf—but William and Charlotte both said no.

'Not until we've proved it,' said Charlotte. 'With the footprint.'

'I've put the sand down,' said William. 'It's just a question of waiting till hc trcads in it.'

Mash wanted to know how they were going to be sure it was the Jogger who had trodden in it and not someone else. Charlotte said they would just have to keep watch. They could take it in turns to hide in the yew hedge. She said she would take the first turn, from five o'clock till six (the Jogger never arrived home before five o'clock), then Mash could take over for an hour, then William.

'And what happens after that?' said Mash. 'If he's still not home?'

'Then we start again,' said Charlotte.

Mash did some calculations on his fingers.

'That means, if he didn't come back till late, I could be sitting out there at ten o'clock!'

'We're sleuths,' said William. 'That's what being a sleuth is all about.

'I can't come out at ten o'clock!' said Mash. 'My dad puts the lock on the door.'

'You could always climb out the window,' said William.

Mash said the windows didn't open: his father had nailed them shut.

'What about the bathroom?' said Charlotte.

Mash said the bathroom window didn't open, either. His father had nailed that shut, as well.

'Kitchen?' said Charlotte.

Mash looked unhappy.

'He must have an obsession,' said Charlotte.

Mr Khan wasn't the only one to have an obsession. As soon as tea was over Gavin insisted that William and Sue went up to the attics to help him hammer the plank of wood across the skylight. This meant clearing the table in Gavin's study, dragging the table onto the landing, placing a chair on top of the table, Gavin getting up onto the chair, Sue and William balancing together as best they could on what little space there was left and supporting the plank of wood with a broom handle while Gavin hammered.

It wasn't very successful. Twice Gavin hit his thumb instead of the nail, and once he fell off the chair and banged his head on the corner of the table.

By the time the plank was finally secured ('This is horrible!' cried Sue. 'It's like living in a fall-out shelter!') it was ten minutes to eight and very nearly time for William to go and take his turn hiding in the yew hedge. Charlotte had called round at six o'clock, after handing over to Mash, to report that nothing had happened. She said that Chalky had come out and gone roaring off in his Thunderbird but the Jogger hadn't yet put in an appearance. He presumably still hadn't, or William would have heard.

'C'n I go now?' He looked pointedly at Gavin. 'I got things to do.'

'I see you've conveniently forgotten about my chapter,' said Gavin.

'Chapter?' Sue sounded alarmed. 'What chapter? You surely haven't finished another one already?'

Gavin said no, he hadn't, that was the whole point—he couldn't get on with it until William had gone downstairs and put his hand through the letter box and discovered whether or not he could open the door without a key.

'Oh!' Sue relaxed. 'I thought you meant you wanted to read us something.' She smiled, brightly. 'Off you go, then, William, and put your hand through the letter box for your father!'

Scowling, William allowed himself to be frog-marched down the stairs.

'I hope this isn't going to take too long,' he said. 'I'm busy.'

'Won't take five seconds!' Gavin assured him.

It was while William was stuck (literally) with his hand in the letter box, and Gavin had gone back upstairs to hunt for the Vaseline before ringing the Fire Brigade, that Mash came prancing down the Terrace.

'Come quick!' mouthed Mash. 'He's here!'

William heaved and jerked. This was an emergency—he couldn't wait for the Fire Brigade!

'Where is he?'

'He's gone indoors with some boxes.' Mash, in his eagerness, was hopping from foot to foot. 'He drove up and opened his boot and there were these big boxes in there. Do you think they're for smuggling the lead?'

'Dunno,' said William. (First things first. Do not allow yourself to be sidetracked.) 'Let's go have a look for the footprint.'

The footprint was there, in the sand, at the foot of the steps. Clean and clear, an exact copy of the one they had found at the scene of the crime. They stood staring at it, marvelling at its perfection, lost in wonderment and a sense of pride ... Their footprint, that they had got! The police couldn't get one; but they had!

'Quick!' said William. 'Before he comes back!'

There wasn't time for making a flour-and-water cast, but William was able to measure it—it was twenty-eight by ten centimetres precisely—and

Mash did a quick sketch. The sketch looked like this:

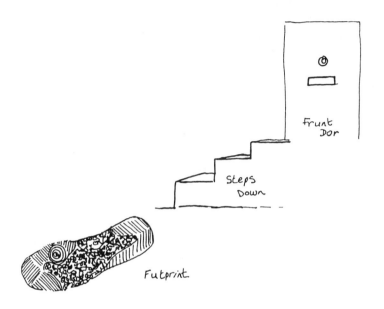

Almost the very second that Mash had finished, something large and heavy came careering down the steps towards them—it was a wooden crate. They jumped clear just in time. The crate came to rest, bang, crash, on top of the footprint, obliterating it entirely. (They couldn't decide, later, whether the crate had been hurled at them, in an attempt to do away with them, or whether it had been hurled at the footprint, with the deliberate intent of destroying the evidence.)

At the top of the steps stood the Jogger.

87

'What do you two kids think you're messing about at? If you've been touching my car—' He raised his fist, threateningly.

'Haven't been near your car,' said William; and as they ran away he shouted over his shoulder, 'Wouldn't touch it with a barge pole!'

Up in the sanctuary of Charlotte's attic they discussed what had happened. Mash said he was sure that he had seen sheets of lead in the wooden crate, and William agreed that it had certainly been heavy enough to contain lead. Charlotte said that in that case, it probably had.

There could be no doubting, now, that the Jogger was the tea-leaf; even Charlotte and William agreed that the evidence was conclusive. The only problem was how to set about proving it?

'I thought this was proof!' cried Mash, waving his drawing of the footprint.

'It's proof to *us*,' said Charlotte. 'But that's only 'cos we know who it b'longs to. The p'lice don't.'

'But it's his shoe!' said Mash. 'His jogging shoe!'

'Yeah, and he's prob'ly busy burning it right now!'

Mash looked glum. 'So what do we do?'

'Have to set a trap,' said William.

That was what Alistair and co. had done in *The Mystery of the Missing Millionaire*. They had set a trap to prove that the millionaire had never really been missing at all.

All they had to do was think of how to do it.

8

Next morning, at breakfast, Sue and Gavin had a row. The thing that started it off was the plank which Gavin had nailed over the attic skylight. Sue wanted it to come down: Gavin wanted it to stay up.

'I'm not leaving myself open to every Tom, Dick and Harry who fancies doing a quick B and E job!'

'What's B and E?' said William.

'And I'm not living here in the pitch black like some kind of troglodyte!' snapped Sue.

'What's a troglodyte?' said William.

'A creature that lives under a stone and never sees daylight, and if you think I'm going to live like that for the next six months—'

'Oh, so it's six months now, is it? Yesterday it was only a couple of weeks . . . another couple of weeks and we'll be rehoused, you said.'

'So we would,' retorted Sue, 'if it weren't for you being so damn choosy!'

'I'm entitled to be choosy!'

'What's B and E?' said William.

'Why you can't go to Monksfield, the same as everyone else—'

'I wouldn't go to Monksfield if it were the last place on earth!'

'Oh, don't be so snooty!'

'What's B and—'

'There is nothing snooty,' hissed Gavin, 'in wishing for a modicum of normal peace and quiet. I cannot work,' said Gavin, lashing himself up, 'in a constant cacophony of dogs barking, kids screeching, babies squalling, women clacking, and mindless maniacs revving up their engines outside my window! I am a creative artist,' bellowed Gavin, 'and I need peace! Do you hear me? PEACE!'

'All right,' said Sue. 'There's no need to shout. We'll get double glazing.'

'If you think,' snarled Gavin, 'that I am going to exist in some hermetically sealed box—'

'Why not? It's what you're doing now? Nailing filthy great lumps of wood all over the windows ... who in their right mind is going to try breaking and entering in Tettiscombe grotty Terrace? What for goodness sake is there to break and enter *for*? And don't tell me your precious manuscript! I am up to here,' said Sue, plonking a hand on top of her head, 'with you and your manuscripts! If I hear any more about your manuscripts I shall go stark mad and start screaming!'

She already was; so was Gavin. William stood stolidly at the gas stove, cooking his holy ghost. Sue and Gavin didn't row very often, but when they did it tended to be violent. Sometimes they threw things. Sue had once thrown her purse at Gavin and it had gone right through the window and never been seen again. Sue had said afterwards that it hardly mattered since there hadn't been anything in it. That, apparently, had been the whole cause of the trouble.

Today the cause of the trouble seemed to be not so much the plank of wood nailed across the window, which is what it had seemed at first, as the fact that Gavin wouldn't go and live on the Monksfield Estate and Sue was worried that very soon they would be the only family left in the Terrace.

'Alec Masterson's moving out on Saturday.'

William, standing at the stove, pricked his ears up.

'Before you know it, everybody will have gone except us.'

'Where's he going?' said William.

'Somewhere posh. Miles away. The other side of town. Of course, he can afford to,' said Sue. 'He's got a proper job.'

'If you're insinuating that writing books is not a proper job—'

They were off again. Thoughtfully, William took his two bits of ghost from under the grill, buttered them while they were still hot, and made a hasty exit before Gavin could grab him to help nail another plank or stick his hand through any more letter boxes. If the Jogger were moving out on Saturday, to somewhere posh that was miles away, then they didn't have much time. They would have to put their plan into operation straight away.

William marched up the steps of number three and rang the bell marked Richardson. He rang the emergency signal—brr, brr, brr-brr-brr. Brr, brr, brr-brr—

Upstairs, a window opened and Mrs Richardson's head looked out.

'You want the girls? They'll be right down!'

He didn't particularly want Geraldine. Seven was too young; you didn't have any sense when you were only seven (not unless you were Spickanspan, the walking wonder child) but there wasn't any escaping it—where Charlotte went, Geraldine went too. And, of course, Boy. Boy was the first down, nose a-glisten, eyes bright, in eager anticipation of another bone hunt. Charlotte and Geraldine came clattering after.

'What is it?' said Charlotte. 'What's happened?'

William jerked his head.

'Got to act fast. He's doing a bunk—Saturday morning. Moving out. I'll get Mash, see you round the back.'

Round the back, beneath the chestnut tree (it had stopped raining, but the ground was still damp) they settled down to work out what Alistair called 'strategy'; which is to say, William, Mash and Charlotte settled down, while Boy went off to uncover his bone and Geraldine sat on a branch and kicked her legs and sang dotty songs to herself.

'The plan will have to be put into operation immediate,' said William. 'What we got to decide—'

'—uffitty huffitty tumtittitoo,' carolled Geraldine, kicking her legs.

'—what we got to decide,' said William, speaking a little louder, 'is how to organize it.'

The first part of the plan was fairly simple—they were going to lay a trap. It was after they had laid it that the difficulties arose. There were two difficulties, mainly—one was Mr Khan locking and bolting his doors and windows so that Mash couldn't get out of the house after ten o'clock at night, and the other was Gavin nailing planks of wood across the skylight so that William couldn't keep a watch for tea-leaves walking on the roof.

They solved both problems in the end by deciding that Mash should ask Mr Khan if he could spend the night with William, and William would ask if he could spend the night with Mash; they would then both go up to Charlotte's attic and hide themselves.

'Let's make a list,' urged Mash.

'List of what?'

'List of what we're going to do right from the beginning.'

The list of what they were going to do right from the beginning looked like this:

5 o'clock	William lies in wait for the Jogger. Mash and Charlotte stay under the chestnut tree.
6 o'clock	Mash takes over from William. William stays with Charlotte.
7 o'clock	Charlotte takes over from Mash. Mash stays with William.

8 o'clock   William takes over from Charlotte.
                Mash stays under the chestnut tree.
                Charlotte goes indoors.

'My mum'll do her nut if I'm not in by eight
... but when it's my turn again I can climb out
the bathroom window and come down the fire
escape.'

They were hoping that long before eight
o'clock the Jogger would have arrived home;
then as soon as they had laid their trap they
could smuggle themselves up to Charlotte's
attic and, as Alistair would have said, 'await
developments'.

A day had never passed so slowly as that
one. There wasn't any more detective work
they could do until the evening, but now that
they had become so used to being busy, to doing
things of meaning and importance, anything
else, such as digging for bodies, or going up
to the adventure playground, seemed childish
and rather silly. William was beginning to understand how it was that Alistair and co. grew
restless when they didn't have a constant supply
of mysteries to solve. Life was going to be very
tame once they'd caught the tea-leaf.

They spent the morning practising. First Charlotte went off to hide in the yew hedge (lying in
wait for the Jogger) whilst William and Mash
waited beneath the chestnut tree. After a few
minutes, from round the side of the Terrace,
they heard a high-pitched squeaking. That was
Charlotte, squeaking one of Boy's squeaky toys

(one of the few he hadn't chewed to pieces). It was the signal that the Jogger had arrived.

Instantly, William and Mash moved up to give support. They found Geraldine, self-importantly playing the part of the Jogger, getting out of an imaginary car, closing the car door, going round to open the boot. In a loud voice Charlotte said, 'Evening, Mr Masterson.'

'Go away!' shrieked Geraldine, being the Jogger. 'What do you want?'

'Thought you'd be int'rested to know that the p'lice have caught the tea-leaf . . . caught him down the buildings, helping himself to sand.'

'Just got to him in time,' said William, 'before he could get back on the roof and nick the rest of that lead.'

'Rest of the lead's still up there,' said Charlotte. 'All rolled up and waiting.'

'Doesn't matter now,' said William. 'Not now they've caught the tea-leaf.'

'I hear the p'lice have called off the search.'

'That's right. They have.'

'Not going to be keeping an eye on us no more.'

'Don't need to now. Don't 'spec there's any more tea-leaves around.'

There was a pause.

'Well, say something,' said Charlotte, prodding Geraldine in the ribs.

Geraldine jerked at an imaginary boot lid and let her hand fly up and slap her in the face.

'Damn an' blars!' roared Geraldine. 'Now look what you made me do!'

After lunch, Mash had to help his mother

with the shopping. Charlotte (pulling a face) said that she and Geraldine were being taken into Tettiscombe to buy winter clothes for school. They arranged to meet again under the chestnut tree at five o'clock.

William spent the afternoon standing on the front door step poking sticks and bits of bent wire through the letter box, with Gavin crouched on the other side shouting encouragement—'That's it, that's it! Bit more to the right . . . down a bit . . . up a bit—'

They didn't succeed in opening the door, but Gavin suddenly had a much better idea, anyway—he would make Alistair take a wax impression of the keyhole.

It pleased him enormously. He was almost jovial as they sat down at four o'clock to eat buttered crumpets. William, seizing the moment, said, 'Is it all right if I go and stay with Mash to-night?' And instead of wanting to know 'Why?' or telling him that he would have to ask his mother, Gavin said, '*May* I go and stay with Mash tonight, of course you may go and stay with Mash tonight. I'm all in favour of encouraging good race relations. An excellent idea!'

William didn't know anything about race relations (what *were* race relations—people you ran races with?), but he did know about taking advantage of Gavin being in a good mood. He galloped up to the attics, grabbed his pyjamas and his dressing-gown, fetched his toothbrush from the bathroom, some carrots and a bag of crisps from the kitchen, stuffed them in a plastic carrier bag and ran. The thing about Gavin's moods was that they could change from one minute to the next and he didn't want to take any chances.

Under the chestnut tree he sat and ate his carrots (he was keeping the crisps in reserve—it could be a long night) and waited for the others. At half-past four Mash arrived, looking agitated.

'My mother won't let me come and stay with you unless your mother writes a note . . . she says it wouldn't be polite for me to come without a proper invitation.'

William chomped his way down a stick of carrot. What would Alistair do?

He knew what Alistair would do. 'Just have to write one ourselves,' he said.

'But that's forgery!' said Mash.

'So what?' In *The Mystery of the Runaway Train* Alistair had written a letter pretending to come from the head of MI5. If Alistair could do it, William didn't see why he couldn't. He flung the stub of his carrot into the undergrowth.

'Let's go and do it quick before Sue gets in.'

On a sheet of Sue's pink writing paper, William wrote his note.

'Dear Mrs Khan,' he wrote, 'Please could Mash come and stay the night with William? Thank you very much, Yours sincerely, Sue Potter. PS Just bring his pijjarmers.'

He wasn't too sure about the spelling of pyjamas, but Mash said it didn't matter as his mother couldn't read English anyway.

'S'what have I gone and written this note for?' said William.

'So that I can read it to her,' said Mash.

The note obviously worked, for ten minutes later Mash turned up under the chestnut tree clutching a plastic carrier bag of his own. Fifteen minutes after that, Charlotte appeared with Boy; and promptly at five o'clock William went off to hide in the yew hedge.

He hoped they wouldn't have to wait too long for the Jogger to arrive. For one thing it wasn't very comfortable, scrunched up inside a yew hedge (yew hedges tended to be prickly) and for another it was boring.

He had just finished counting sheep up as far as ten thousand and was in the middle of going through the alphabet thinking of makes of car—Alvis, Bentley, Cadillac, Datsun—when there was a screeching of brakes and Chalky's Thunderbird came rocketing to a halt just in front of him.

William watched, through the branches, as Chalky got out and went round to open the bonnet. It was while Chalky was doing things with the engine that the Jogger's Fiat drove up. The Jogger also got out. He, too, went round to open the bonnet.

William watched impatiently from inside the hedge, waiting for Chalky to finish and go indoors, but Chalky showed no signs of finishing. He had obviously found something of interest—something that needed investigating.

William chewed at a fingernail. Any minute now and it would be the Jogger who went indoors. None of their plans had allowed for the possibility of someone else being there.

The good sleuth, Alistair had once said, must always be prepared to adapt.

Very well! He would adapt.

William turned—as best you *can* turn, in the middle of a yew hedge—and burrowed his way further along until he came level with Chalky's Thunderbird. Carelessly, trying to look as if he had just strolled in from the street, he emerged.

'Hallo, John!' Chalky looked up, surprised. 'Where you sprung from?'

William waved a hand, vaguely, in the direction of Tettiscombe Grove.

'Just checking the old jam jar,' said Chalky. 'Want to have a gander?'

At any other time William would have been only too happy. This evening, he had other things on his mind. As he bent over the engine, side by side with Chalky, he said loudly, 'I hear the p'lice caught that tea-leaf, then.'

'What tea-leaf's that, John?'

'One that's bin nicking all our lead.'

'Oh, yeah?' Chalky leaned forward, doing things with a spanner. 'So where'd they catch him?'

'Caught him down the building site, trying to nick sand.'

'Oh, yeah?'

Chalky's voice was muffled inside the engine.

'Yeah.' William glanced up. The Jogger had taken out his handkerchief and was energetically polishing at something, pretending not to listen. 'I reckon they got to him just about in time.'

'Yeah?'

''Fore he had a chance to get back on the roof.'

'Oh! Yeah.'

'Rest of the lead's still up on that roof. Course—' William gazed across at the Jogger, still polishing with his handkerchief, still pretending not to listen —'they've stopped watching the place now. No point any more . . . not now they've caught him. After all, I don't expect there's any other tea-leaves around.'

The Jogger suddenly closed his bonnet with a bang. He gave a snickering laugh.

'I wouldn't be so sure of that,' sneered the Jogger, 'if I were you.'

9

'So tell us again what he said?'

'*I* said, I don't expect there's any more tea-leaves around, an' *he* said, I wouldn't be so sure of that if I were you.'

'Cool!' said Charlotte. 'Dead cool!'

They were up in Charlotte's attic; William and Mash, Charlotte, Geraldine and Boy. Mrs Richardson didn't know that William and Mash were up there. Charlotte had smuggled them up while the sitting-room door was closed and her parents were watching television. The plan was that as soon as footsteps were heard on the attic stairs, Mash and William would crawl into the narrow space between the bed and the wall and stop breathing.

At ten o'clock, the footsteps came. William and Mash dived for cover. Just in time! Seconds later, the door opened and Mrs Richardson looked round.

'You two asleep?' she said.

Grunt, went Charlotte.

Whiffle, went Geraldine.

Tickle went the dust from the attic floor up

William's nose.

William held his breath. He had read somewhere that if you concentrated extra hard you could actually stop yourself from sneezing.

The door closed.

Aaaaaaaaaaaah-TCHOO! went William and Mash, in chorus.

They froze; but the seconds ticked past and nothing happened.

'It's all right,' whispered Charlotte. 'They'll be going to bed soon.'

It was dark by now, so instead of taking it in turns to listen for footsteps they took it in turns to sit on the landing, on Charlotte's bedroom stool, staring up at the skylight. There was only one route the Jogger could take, and that was straight across the roof, which meant he would have to pass directly overhead.

It was quite creepy, sitting on the landing. The house was all in darkness, except for a dim light burning in the hall, two floors below. They couldn't even talk, except in whispers, for fear of waking Charlotte's parents.

William sighed, and looked at his new digital luminous watch (a present from his grandmother, who had got it with her petrol). It said twenty to twelve. Surely, if the Jogger intended coming back for the rest of the lead, he would do it by midnight?

If he intended coming back. If he didn't come tonight—

CRUMP.

William jumped. What was that?

There it was again ... CRUMP. CRUMP. CRUMP.

Someone was on the roof! A shadow was moving across the skylight—feet were running over it! Clump clonk clunk they went, directly overhead.

It was the moment they had been waiting for. William streaked for the attic—where everybody, including Boy, had gone to sleep.

'Pst!' He shook at Charlotte, making vigorous pointing motions towards the ceiling as he did so.

Charlotte woke immediately, and got the message. She nodded and reached out for Boy's lead, whilst William prodded at Mash. Mash was harder to wake—he had to be prodded three times.

Geraldine wasn't prodded at all, because they had decided not to take her. She was going to be furious when she woke up and discovered; but as William had said, and as Charlotte for once had agreed, seven years old just wasn't old enough to go chasing tea-leaves. Not at dead of night. Even Spickanspan, the boy genius, had to be left behind on occasion.

Down the stairs they stole, William behind Charlotte, Mash behind William. It was just like creeping down the stairs at number three, except that in number three William knew exactly which steps had to be trodden on carefully so as to avoid creaking and which had to be missed out altogether. In Charlotte's place it was Charlotte who knew, so that every now and again she would turn and point and shake

103

her head, and William would do likewise to Mash.

They left the house by the back door. The bolts were rather stiff (Alistair, of course, would have oiled them beforehand: Alistair always thought of *every*thing) but they managed them at last, after much struggling and heaving.

Outside, the garden looked more junglelike than ever. The moonlight made strange shapes of things, so that boa constrictors hung in loops from the branches of trees, and wild animals crouched ready to spring. It was just as well they hadn't brought Geraldine. At seven years old you would probably be scared. At eleven you realized that of course it *was* only the moonlight.

By the steps of number two they hid and waited. The minutes passed; then suddenly, on the edge of the roof, in clear silhouette against the moonlit sky, a figure appeared. It seemed to be wrestling with something. Something large, and heavy, like—

'Watch out!' hissed Charlotte.

They hurled themselves out of the way just in time. With a loud THUD, something large and heavy hit the steps of number three. Another second, and they would all have been crushed.

'What is it?' gasped Mash.

William opened his mouth to say, 'Lead,' but before he could get any further than 'L—' there was another muffled thud, this time from somewhere inside the Terrace. Boy gave a warning growl, and Charlotte quickly smothered his muzzle with her hand. Mash shivered, even though it wasn't cold.

'What was *that*?'

William swallowed. 'I dunno.'

'Do you think it was a bomb?'

'I dunno.'

'If it was a bomb, we oughtn't to be here. We—'

'Quiet!' said Charlotte. 'Keep to the plan!'

The plan was that they should wait for the Jogger to come round the back and collect his booty, then jump on him, pin him to the ground and squash him in the mud, whilst one of them went to fetch the police.

'So where is he?' said Mash, agitated. 'Where has he gone?'

Silently, Charlotte pointed. Up on the roof, a figure had come into sight, heaving and tugging at a second roll of lead. They could hear the lead scraping and grinding as slowly the tea-leaf dragged it towards the edge. It seemed to be giving him trouble, for after a bit he broke off and pressed both hands into the small of his back, as if he had pulled a muscle; then he stopped and tried picking it up, but it was obviously too heavy, for he let it fall again, with a thump, and after a few seconds started back on his hauling.

Down behind the wall, they watched and waited. It was just as well they hadn't brought Geraldine. This sort of thing was far too danger-ous for a seven-year-old. For all they knew, the tea-leaf could be armed. He could be a hardened criminal, sought by the police of ten countries. He could—

'What's that?' yelped Mash, grabbing at William.

William looked. His blood froze. Wraithlike, across the gardens, a white blob was floating.

It was Geraldine, in her night-dress.

Mash relaxed his grip on William. Charlotte relaxed her grip on Boy.

'What are you doing here?' she said, crossly.

'There was a noise,' said Geraldine, 'and I woke up. And you weren't there, so I came to find you, and I think you're horrid meany pigs to go off like that without telling me and I hate you for it, and there's a car with policemen coming down the road and your dad—' she nodded at William—'is standing in the street in his pyjamas waving at them.'

'P'lice!' Charlotte turned, accusingly, on William. 'Your dad's gone and got the p'lice!'

Abruptly, as they watched, the figure on the roof gave up his struggle with the lead. Dropping it where it was, he turned and went tearing back across the skylights, heading for the safety of number one.

'Quick!' screeched Charlotte. 'Head him off! We got to get to him before the p'lice!'

Through the jungle they pounded, over the wall, out into the open. Too late! Even as they rounded the side of the Terrace, two policemen in uniform, followed by Gavin in his pyjamas, went streaming up the steps of number three.

'Knickers!' shouted Charlotte.

At that moment, the front door of number one

opened and Chalky appeared. William rushed up.

'You seen the tea-leaf?'

'Yeah, he's up there.' Chalky jerked a thumb. 'I laid one on him. Can't stop, got to get Old Bill!'

'Old Bill's already—' began William, but Chalky didn't hear him. He was off and away.

Charlotte threw her arms into the air: 'Now we'll get *two* lots of p'lice!'

'Maybe,' said Mash, nervously, 'we should just give up and—'

'Give up?' shrieked Charlotte. 'After it's us that's done all the hard work?'

William suddenly felt masterful. He felt how Alistair must feel: cool, fearless, and in command.

'You lot stay here,' he said. 'I'm going in.'

'What for?' said Charlotte.

'Guard the body.' That way, they could at least lay claim to some of the honour and glory, even though in the end it had been Chalky who had actually captured the tea-leaf. Not that William minded sharing with Chalky. Chalky was his mate. 'You wait outside and be ready to jump on him,' he said. 'Just in case.'

'Case what?'

'Case anything goes wrong.'

It was hard to see what could. If Chalky said he had laid one on him, then knowing Chalky he would have made a good job of it. Chalky had been itching to lay one on the Jogger for a long time.

William had just reached the second landing when from the floor below he heard what sounded like a door opening.

'Hey, you!'

He froze.

'You up there! What's going on? What's all the commotion? Answer me!'

Slowly, prepared for instant flight, William inched forward to the head of the stairs. Down below, looking angrily up, dressed in silly little short pyjamas covered all over in pink flowers, with his hair sticking out in spikes, stood the Jogger.

The *Jogger???*

How had he got there? He was supposed to be lying upstairs, unconscious! Chalky had laid one on him. He couldn't possibly have had time to come to his senses, get back to his bedroom, change into his silly little short pyjamas—

'What's the matter, you? Are you deaf?'

Losing patience, the Jogger stalked off to the front door. William stood, mesmerized, watching him go.If it wasn't the Jogger that Chalky had laid one on, then who was it?

William turned, and went galloping on, up the stairs. Up the second flight, up the third, up to the attics—where was it? WHERE WAS THE BODY? The body had gone!

At that moment the skylight was thrown violently open and two policemen came bursting through. The first one, despite landing almost on top of him, ignored William completely and went charging off down the stairs. The second shouted, 'Out of my way, sunshine!' and went charging off after him.

After a second's startled pause, William set off in pursuit.

Back down the stairs they hurtled. Down the second flight, down the first, down the steps and crash bang wallop into the flattened figure of the Jogger, being sat on in the mud . . .

10

'Not very clever, you kids! Obstructing the course of justice.'

The constable regarded them, severely. They stood in a row before him—Charlotte, William and Mash, with Geraldine tacked on at the end and Boy, one leg stuck up in the air, inspecting himself for fleas.

'I shall recommend you be given a good talking to! You have behaved highly irresponsibly. If it hadn't been for you,' said the constable, 'we might well have laid our hands on the villain. Now! What have you to say for yourselves?'

Charlotte scowled, and didn't say anything. Mash looked at his feet. Geraldine, who didn't count, was plaiting her hair; and William, for his part, was still trying to puzzle out what had gone wrong.

One of the things that had gone wrong was that Gavin's plank of wood which he had nailed across the skylight had broken loose and crashed all the way down the attic stairs. That was what had caused the bang they had heard, and the noise which had woken Geraldine.

It had also woken Gavin, who, in his panic, imagining it to be someone coming to murder them, had instantly rushed to the telephone and summoned the police.

That was one of the things that had gone wrong.

Another of the things that had gone wrong was that Charlotte and Boy, aided and abetted by Geraldine and Mash, had squashed an innocent citizen face down in the mud and sat on him.

Just to make matters worse, while they had been squashing the innocent citizen in the mud, the tea-leaf had been jumping into his Thunderbird and making his getaway.

William heaved a sigh. It wasn't the Jogger that Chalky had laid one on. Chalky hadn't laid one on anybody. That had all been part of his diabolical cunning, like letting his own attic get rained on. That was the most diabolically cunning thing William had ever heard of. It had thrown them right off the scent.

At least it was a solace to know that they had been up against a real master criminal and not just some petty crook. He bet even Alistair would have been taken in by Chalky.

Well, perhaps not Alistair, because Alistair was never taken in by anyone; but he'd jolly well like to know how he would have guessed!

Of course, there had been that bit right at the beginning when it was Chalky who'd told William about the tea-leaf, and Gavin had said how come Chalky knew about it when the police had only spoken to him and Mrs Richardson.

But then there was the footprint. He still didn't understand—

Suddenly, it came to him. The footprint! It had been staring them in the face, right there in Mash's drawing.

The footprint had been pointing away from the house. But the Jogger, at that stage, had not yet come out of the house. The Jogger had gone *in*. It was Chalky who had come out . . .

'I can only trust,' said the constable, fixing William with a stern eye, 'that you have learnt something by this experience.'

William had certainly learnt something. What William had learnt was that the last thing you could expect was gratitude. If this was all the thanks you got, then he was through with detective work. They could jolly well manage without him in future. They didn't seem to realize that if it hadn't been for him and the others setting a trap, Chalky wouldn't have been up on the roof tonight in the first place.

He was glad they hadn't caught him. He might be a tea-leaf, but he was still William's mate. As for that Jogger—

A blissful smile slowly spread itself across William's features. Pink-flowered pyjamas . . . blimey, what a sight!

SOME OTHER NEW WINDMILLS
YOU WILL ENJOY

RED SKY IN THE MORNING

Elizabeth Laird

Anna is a happy, sensitive girl whose cares and concerns are those of any teenager, until her brother, Ben, is born physically and mentally handicapped. At first Anna is confused, she loves Ben yet cannot bring herself to tell her friends about him, and he has a turbulent effect on her family. Yet these difficulties are overcome through the love and tenderness Ben generates, leaving the reader with a strong sense of the positive contribution he makes to the family.

Winner of the Burnley Express Children's Books of the Year Award. Shortlisted for the Carnegie medal and The Children's Book Award.

ISBN: 0 435 12355 6

THE ROAD AHEAD

Lois Lowry

Twelve-year-old Rabble lives with her mother over a garage belonging to 'the Bigelows' – her mother is their housekeeper. When Mrs Bigelow is taken into hospital and Rabble and her mother move into the house with Mr. Bigelow and his daughter, Rabble feels she is finally living with a real family. But she knows her 'family' is temporary and she will have to move on . . .

ISBN: 0 435 12356 4

MY FAMILY AND OTHER ANIMALS

Gerald Durrell

'"Don't be ridiculous, dear" said mother firmly; "that's quite out of the question. It would be madness."

So we sold our house and fled from the gloom of the English Summer like a flock of migrating swallows.'

Carrying only what they consider to be 'the bare essentials of life the Durrell family arrive in sun-soaked Corfu, and so begin the much-loved tales of Gerald Durrell's early life with "My Family and other animals"'.

ISBN: 0 435 12354 8

MY FRIEND WALTER

Michael Morpurgo

When a mysterious invitation lands on the doorstep. Bess is the only family member who attends a reunion in London. But Bess's visit to London is just the start of a series of unusual events. Who is the stranger in the black cloak who is so keen to talk to her? And how can Bess hide her friendly ghost from the family in Devon? And is there a connection between their friendship and the disappearance of the crown jewels? The ghost proves to be a disturbing and important influence on the lives of all the family.

This exciting and humorous adventure story by a highly-acclaimed writer of children's books is a must for the classroom.

ISBN: 0 435 12362 9

RICE WITHOUT RAIN

Minfong Ho

Jinda lives with her family in a Thai village which gives up half of its rice crop to landowners – until students from Bangkok University incite the villagers to rebel. The student intervention brings romance for Jinda, but bloody consequences for the village.

A sensitive exploration of a young girl coming to terms with the demands of love, family loyalty and politics.

ISBN: 0 435 12340 8

THE WOODS AT THE END OF AUTUMN STREET
Lois Lowry

Elizabeth senses there is something to be afraid of in the woods at the end of Autumn Street. Yet she cannot put a name to these shadowy fears. In fact she cannot put a name to many of the bewildering things in the adult world – the anxiety she senses in the "whispers between adults", why her father had to go away because of the war and why her friend Charles cannot go everywhere with her just because he is black. Yet Elizabeth loves her friendship with the warm, street-wise Charles and together they interpret the mysteries around them. Until the fatal day the adult world intrudes all too violently into their childhood . . . .

ISBN: 0 435 12352 1

THE GOLDEN APPLES
OF THE SUN

Ray Bradbury

The captain who takes a rocket to the sun to bring back a cup full of sunlight. The girl looking for love who travels through a balmy spring night into bodies not her own. The women about to leave earth to join their husbands on Mars. The panic-stricken man who becomes a murderer by accident. These are just some of the characters in this scintillating collection of stories from the century's most popular fantasy writer.

ISBN: 0 435 12360 2

THE DIARY OF ANNE FRANK

Anne Frank

Anne Frank was given a diary for her thirteenth birthday – her favourite present and her best friend. Writing came easily to her and in her astonishingly intimate records we learn of her strength and tolerance as she faced the strains of hiding in sealed-off rooms from the Nazi invaders.

The Diary of Anne Frank will be an excellent text to offer pupils aiming for level 7 and above of the National Curriculum, who will be reading a range of literature including autobiography.

ISBN: 0 435 12363 7